Dogmagic

Also by Holly Webb

Catmagic

Dogmagic

HOLLY WEBB

SCHOLASTIC

First published in the UK in 2008 by Scholastic Children's Books
An imprint of Scholastic Ltd
Euston House, 24 Eversholt Street
London, NW1 1DB, UK
Registered office: Westfield Road, Southam, Warwickshire, CV47 0RA
SCHOLASTIC and associated logos are trademarks and or registered trademarks of
Scholastic Inc.

Text copyright © Holly Webb, 2008

The right of Holly Webb to be identified as the author
of this work has been asserted by her.

ISBN 978 1 407 10597 0

A CIP catalogue record for this book
is available from the British Library

Printed by CPI Bookmarque, Croydon, CR0 4TD
Papers used by Scholastic Children's Books are made from wood
grown in sustainable forests.

3 5 7 9 10 8 6 4

www.scholastic.co.uk/zone

For Jon, Tom, Robin and William

1

Lottie Grace buttoned up her new red school cardigan, and peered into the wardrobe mirror hopefully. It wasn't *too* bad.

"That is too big, that red . . . jumper thing," said a prissy little voice with a definite French accent.

Lottie turned back from the mirror to see Sofie frowning at her, her dark muzzle wrinkled disapprovingly. The little dog liked her to be properly dressed.

"Cardigan. Yes, I know. Uncle Jack got it all from that tiny school uniform shop down the road, and I don't think he got the sizes quite right. It's a good thing I already had shoes from my other school. I just wish we were allowed to wear trousers at Netherbridge Hill, like we could there. This skirt is grim." Lottie held out the grey fabric disgustedly.

"Twirl," Sofie demanded. She was perched on Lottie's bed, watching like a fashion journalist at a catwalk show. She sniffed. "Well, as you say, it *could* be worse. At least red is a good colour with your dark

1

hair." She jumped down and padded round Lottie. "I could accidentally bite it for you if you like, this skirt. It is not *chic*."

"Then I'd probably just have to go to school in a torn skirt, Sofie. I can't see Uncle Jack buying me another one; he'd know you did it on purpose." She scooped Sofie up, getting black dachshund hairs all over the new cardigan, but not caring.

Every time Lottie held Sofie now, a thrill of happiness went through her. It had been only two weeks since she and Sofie had discovered the magical bond they had with each other. With Sofie as her familiar, Lottie felt like she could do almost anything. Having Sofie's confidence and snappish French common sense almost as a part of her was helping a lot with her worries about her new school.

Lottie had been living at Grace's Pet Shop for six weeks now. She was supposed to have gone home at the end of the holidays, and back to her old school, but her mum's job in France had been made permanent. If it wasn't for the new school, and missing Mum and her old friends, Lottie wouldn't have minded staying at all. Uncle Jack's shop was the most fabulous place to be. Lottie had loved it from the beginning, even before she knew what it really was. Then she had found out that Grace's Pet Shop was not just your usual pet shop – it sold animals who could talk, and had all sorts of other magical tricks and secrets.

That had been surprising enough, but eventually Uncle Jack had revealed something even more important. The shop had been her home once before. She'd been born there, while her mum and dad still lived in Netherbridge. Her dad, Tom, had been Uncle Jack's partner in the business. And he had been just as magically gifted with animals as Uncle Jack was. Lottie couldn't remember it at all, except for odd flashes of memory here and there – like she'd known there was something strangely familiar about this bedroom with its pink spotty bedclothes and curtains.

When Lottie and her mum and dad had lived here, Lottie's mum hadn't even noticed the magical things happening in the shop. Lottie couldn't really see why not – even before Sofie had let the secret out to her, she'd been seeing and hearing odd things, things that had made her wonder what was going on. How could her mum not have seen them too?

"Lottie!" Her cousin Danny was yelling up the stairs. "Lottie! Phone! It's your mum!"

Lottie and Sofie galloped down the stairs to grab the phone off him.

"Nice *outfit*, Lottie. . ." Danny said, smirking, as he held it out. "Stylish."

Lottie stuck her tongue out at him. "Have you tried yours on yet?" she asked sweetly. "Your dad bought it when he got mine, and I bet he doesn't know your size either. Did he mention 'room to grow' at all?"

Danny looked blank for a moment, then hurtled up the stairs to his room, leaving Lottie giggling and Sofie making amused little whining noises deep in her throat.

"Lottie?" Her mother's voice was calling squeakily from the phone, and Lottie hurriedly sat down on the stairs and put it to her ear.

"Sorry, Mum, I was just talking to Danny."

"That's OK, Lottie, I was just ringing to say good luck for tomorrow."

Lottie grimaced. "Thanks."

"Oh, come on, Lottie, it might be fun!" her mother said hopefully.

Lottie rolled her eyes at Sofie, who was sitting on the step above with her nose resting on Lottie's shoulder. Her mum was always relentlessly cheerful about this sort of thing. Personally, Lottie thought it was a lot better to be a bit pessimistic; then you might get a pleasant surprise. "Mum, I'm not going to know *anyone*. It's like my worst nightmare come true!"

Her mum sighed. "Sorry, Lottie. I was just trying to cheer you up."

"It's OK," Lottie muttered. "It'll probably be fine after a few days." *Please*. . . she thought desperately.

Lottie lay on her bed, nibbling her hair thoughtfully and occasionally sighing at the school uniform hanging on the back of her door. Getting a call from her mum had made Lottie think back to two weeks ago, when she had visited from France. It was the first time her mum had been back to England since her job had moved to Paris, and it had been wonderful. Lottie was still sad that her mum was so far away, but it wasn't so hard to deal with now.

When she and Sofie had first discovered their joined powers, they'd used them to make an incredible, dreamlike trip to Paris to visit her. Lottie had watched longingly through the window of her mum's flat, and seen how much her mum was missing her, and how hard she was trying to look after her. Lottie had hugged her and told her it was OK, and that she understood, but because they were there by magic, Lottie's not-at-all-magical mum hadn't been able to see her. But it was after their visit that she'd arranged the trip back to be with Lottie, so she must have felt something.

It had been weird having her mum at the shop. But the oddest thing was she couldn't see half the animals, and kept asking why all the cages were empty.

Even when the flighty, chatterbox mice forgot to be quiet and had giggly conversations in front of her, she just didn't seem to hear. Or she rubbed her ears, and said she must be tired. The mice found it half funny and half infuriating. Mice are complete attention-seekers, and hate someone ignoring them. They had persuaded Horace, the grumpy old African Grey parrot, to learn Lottie's mum's mobile ringtone and perform it every so often. She was addicted to her phone, and was waiting for several important calls from work, so she would always dive into her bag frantically, and then pull the phone out, looking very confused when the ringing abruptly stopped. When she got as far as ringing the phone company and complaining that her phone was broken, the mice nearly fell out of their cage laughing. They said it was well worth their week's ration of sunflower seeds that Horace had demanded in payment.

Surprisingly, Mum had got on really well with Ariadne, Uncle Jack's girlfriend, who also happened to be a witch. Lottie had been really worrying about this – Ariadne was teaching her how to use her magic, and they'd got really close. She so wanted Mum to like her, but she'd thought that Ariadne's witchiness wouldn't go well with Mum's matter-of-fact attitude. Even their clothes were so different. Ariadne was into long, flouncy, gypsy-ish skirts, *lots* of jewellery, and black eyeliner, whereas Lottie's mum lived in trouser suits – or very stylish and well-pressed jeans, if she had to. Lottie's mum had given Ariadne a slightly shocked look when she first met her (Lottie thought it was probably because of the black lace gloves), but after five minutes they'd been chatting quite happily.

Lottie had stared suspiciously at Ariadne when she

heard her mum asking her where she'd got her dangly, black earrings. Mum never wore anything like that! But Ariadne just smiled innocently at her. Lottie was pretty sure she'd reached into her mum's mind, but probably she'd only shaped her thoughts a *little* bit. Ariadne's powers made her a strong mind-reader, and she could *change* people's minds too – though she said it was not something that you should ever do unless they wanted you to, deep down. Lottie's mum had wanted so much to know that Lottie was being looked after, and now she did. . .

Lottie had taken her mum and Sofie on lots of walks round Netherbridge, exploring her favourite places: the park, the river that ran through the centre of the town, and Valentin's, the coffee shop that she and French-born Sofie haunted for hot chocolate, espresso and cakes.

"This is new," her mum had said, looking round admiringly as they sat at a pavement table under the stripy awning. "It used to be a grotty old tea shop, run by the grumpiest, most ancient lady you've ever met." She smiled, remembering. "In fact, she threw us out once, Lottie, because you broke a cup." She shook her head. "I never worked out how it happened, actually; I could have sworn you weren't touching it, but she was muttering on and on about nasty messy little children, and suddenly it was smashed on the floor. We never went back, but it wasn't much of a loss."

Lottie and Sofie exchanged significant glances, and Lottie resolved to ask Ariadne about it. Would she have been able to levitate a cup as a tiny child?

"Have you started drinking coffee, Lottie?" her mum asked in surprise, when she ordered an espresso.

Lottie flushed. She'd done it without thinking. "Oh, no. . . It's for Sofie, Mum. She really loves it. I'd like a hot chocolate, please," she added to the smiling waiter. He adored Sofie, and always brought her extra biscuits.

Mum shook her head, smiling slightly. "That dog really is unbelievably spoilt," she said. "But then Jack was always like that with his animals."

Sofie glared at her, and Mum wilted slightly, and added, "But then she is very sweet too, and obviously intelligent." She looked thoughtfully at Sofie. "It's almost as though she understands, isn't it?"

Sofie looked at Lottie and quite clearly rolled her eyes up in despair. "*Imbécile,*" she muttered, out of the corner of her mouth.

Lottie thought she probably ought to object to that, but really, Mum was unbelievable. . . Besides, from Sofie, *imbécile* was almost a term of endearment. She called Lottie it all the time.

"Does it feel odd being back at the shop, Mum?" she asked, wanting to change the subject.

The coffees arrived just then, and Lottie's mum

stirred hers slowly, half smiling and watching Sofie lap the tiny bubbles from the espresso with her delicate pink tongue. "Yes," she said quietly. "Very odd. It's the first time I've been back since . . . since your father died, Lottie. That place is full of memories."

"Mum," Lottie asked hesitantly, "I know you don't like to talk about it, but what happened to Dad? You've never told me."

Her mother closed her eyes, as though it hurt even to think about it, and Lottie immediately felt sorry for asking. But she didn't want to back down, as she always had before. She stared determinedly at her mum, willing her to answer.

"He was off on a buying trip, for the shop," her mother said quietly. "He and Uncle Jack, they had – probably your uncle still has – a lot of private clients who want more exotic animals. Tropical birds, odd reptiles, that sort of thing. Tom went on a long trip, a month, to the rainforest. He – never came back. . ."

Lottie gasped. "But what happened? Why not?"

"We don't know." Her mum was whispering now. Then her voice grew harder, and louder. "He shouldn't have gone, Lottie. It wasn't fair, with a small child, to go off and leave us. He should have taken better care!" She stopped suddenly, shuddering. "This is why I don't talk about it, Lottie. I'm still too angry, even seven years later." She laughed bitterly. "I said that . . . that I didn't want him to go, and he offered to take us too. He said it would be good for you to see the rainforests before they disappeared. That was so like him. He was a wonderful father, Lottie, he loved you very much, but he wasn't very practical. I had to be the practical one, always." She stared at Lottie, her face pale and sharp. "That's hard, you know. Sometimes it would be nice to say, *Oh, don't worry, let's just do something crazy today*. But I can't. I have to be careful, keep us safe." Mum sighed, and smiled sadly at her. "You do understand, don't you, Lottie?" she asked gently.

Lottie nodded. She had her hands wrapped round her cup of hot chocolate, and it was too hot, but somehow she couldn't put it down. Her mother was still hurting so much, and she'd never realized. She felt desperately sad. Her secret trip to Paris had helped her understand why her mum had felt she had to take the new job. She couldn't bear to think that she might be out of work and not able to look after Lottie. Lottie had thought this was just because her mum was on her own. But these painful words added a whole new dimension to it. She couldn't bear to do anything risky because it made her think of Lottie's dad, disappearing off on his rainforest trip – and not coming back.

2

Lottie trailed slowly up the steep lane that led to Netherbridge Hill Primary School. She'd been past the old-fashioned, swirly black gates a few times on walks with Sofie, but she'd always hurried by, not wanting to think about school, telling herself it was ages away. But the summer holidays had just disappeared – an awful lot had changed in the last six weeks.

It was amazing how many children were swarming towards the school, considering how few people her age she'd seen round Netherbridge over the summer. But Danny had told her that lots of people got a school bus in from the smaller villages around the area. Lottie carefully eyed up everyone else's uniforms. Good. They seemed to fit just as badly as hers did. Clearly the little shop on the high street only did small, medium and "room to grow". Mum had brought her some smart red hairclips that she'd found in a shop in Paris, with cherries on. They were really cute, and Lottie kept touching the clips to make sure they were still in properly. It was nice to have something that no one else would have, and something to remind her of Mum.

The gates were surrounded by younger children saying goodbye to their parents, and Lottie wished for a moment that she'd taken Uncle Jack up on his offer to come with her on the first day. But Danny had snorted with laughter and said, "She's in year six, Dad, not reception! Do you want her to look a complete saddo?"

So that had been that, really. Danny had to catch a bus to the secondary school in the next town now, and he'd left earlier, so she hadn't been able to walk with him either. He hadn't been great company at breakfast, anyway; he was unusually silent. Lottie thought he was probably nervous too, though he was much too proud to admit it.

Lottie threaded her way through the crowd at the gate and slipped into the playground, looking at the school properly for the first time. It was ancient. Her old school had been very new, only built a few years before, and it looked modern and friendly. Lottie had a sudden longing to be with her old mates Rachel and Hannah, walking through their estate, knowing everyone, knowing who her teacher would be, and hearing all the gossip about who'd done what over the summer. This building didn't look like a school. It was more like some sort of grim orphanage in a film, where children got shut up and left. It was very tidy, and the windows sparkled, but that was about all Lottie could see in its favour. Those windows were high up in the classroom walls, to stop people seeing out, and Lottie almost expected to see sad little faces peering out of the bottom panes as the orphans tried to see the outside world. She sighed. This wasn't helping. It was just different, that was all. *Picturesque*, she told herself firmly. It was one of her mum's favourite words.

A teacher was standing in the middle of the playground with a list, trying to shoo people inside, but most of the children were ignoring her and racing around to see their friends. Lottie supposed that if they lived all round the area, they might only see each other at school. She was really glad Uncle Jack lived in Netherbridge itself, not way out in the countryside somewhere. Lottie loved Netherbridge, the way she and Sofie could go out on their own and still feel safe, the pretty, old houses, and the river to wander by. It was nice not to be surrounded by noise and people all the time, like at home. But at the same time, she couldn't imagine living in the middle of nowhere, with just trees and fields to look at.

Ignoring the little voice telling her just to turn round and walk out of the gate again, Lottie walked very slowly over to the harassed-looking teacher, and smiled politely at her. "Hello. I'm Lottie Grace.

I'm new. Could you tell me where I should go, please?"

The teacher was nice, at least. She pointed Lottie in the direction of her classroom, told her where the loos were, and said she was looking forward to getting to know her. Lottie felt almost cheerful. It was amazing what one nice person could do to make you feel better. Unfortunately, she then turned round to go to her classroom, and found Zara and her little clique behind her, all smiling sweetly.

Lottie's stomach turned over. She'd met Zara soon after she came to Netherbridge, and decided within about two minutes of knowing her that she was horrible. Zara knew Danny (he was in the year above her at school, and Lottie was pretty certain she and her mates all fancied him), and she'd heard all the gossip about his cousin who'd been dumped at the pet shop while her mum went off to Paris. She lost no time in making sure Lottie knew her place – at the bottom of the social heap, unwanted, and certainly not welcome.

In a way, Lottie knew, she ought to be grateful to Zara. After that first encounter, desperate to escape from the girls' teasing, Lottie had tried to run the wrong way back to the shop. Sofie had broken her silence to tell her where to go, and the whole secret of the shop had come out.

A week or so later, Lottie and Sofie had found

Zara's gang teasing a stray cat. Lottie had stood up to her in front of everyone to rescue the cat. Lottie didn't think Zara would ever forgive them, especially as Sofie had torn a massive piece out of her very pretty skirt when Zara had tried to kick her. Still, it had definitely been the right thing to do, and the poor, shivering little stray had turned out to be a remarkably powerful creature, and had been adopted by Ariadne as a new familiar, Tabitha. Tabitha and the others couldn't help Lottie now though.

"Hello, Mrs Hartley!" Zara sounded like a model pupil. "Did you have a good summer?"

"Zara! Hello, and hello Ellie and Amy and Bethany. Thank you, yes, it was lovely. Now, girls, you've arrived at just the right time. This is Lottie, and I'm pretty sure ... yes, she is going to be in Mrs Laurence's class with all of you. So could you point her in the right direction? Keep an eye on her?"

"Of course we will," Zara promised, looking wide-eyed and angelic at the unknowing teacher. She even put an arm round Lottie and gave her a little hug. "Hi, Lottie! We'll *definitely* keep an eye on her, Mrs Hartley."

Lottie just bet they would.

Zara was clearly everyone's favourite person at Netherbridge Hill. All the teachers', anyway. Lottie wasn't so sure about the rest of her class. She thought

15

she spotted a few disbelieving looks when Zara gushingly introduced Lottie to Mrs Laurence. Still, she *was* being very nice. Lottie wasn't sure why. She certainly didn't trust her an inch.

It was weird, Lottie mused to herself, sitting where Mrs Laurence had put her, opposite Zara, "since you all seem to be getting on so well!" Zara looked like she ought to be a nice person. She was pretty, but not so much that you'd be jealous of her for it. She had mid-brown hair, very long; large dark-blue eyes; and pink cheeks, a bit like an expensive china doll. She looked – wholesome. Not as though she spent her life alternately charming people and back-stabbing them, which Lottie was pretty sure she did.

Lottie wished that Zara would just cut the act. It was horrible watching her smile, and offer to share her glitter pens so Lottie could decorate her new books. Lottie felt like she was being wound up too tight, and something was going to break any minute. Unless Zara had had some sort of spooky personality transplant in the last couple of weeks, of course. How could anyone actually fake being this nice for so long?

She had to wait all morning, her insides fizzing nervously as she wondered what Zara's plan was. Then Zara's little gang scooped her up with them and headed off to the school hall, which had tables put out in it for lunches. Their fake niceness lasted long enough to advise Lottie not to get the shepherd's pie

("Made with real shepherds. . ." Bethany giggled), but then they bagged a table well away from the dinner ladies and the patrolling teachers and trapped Lottie right by the wall, so she'd have to struggle past all of them to get out.

Lottie stared at her plate, waiting for whatever Zara was planning.

"Aren't you hungry, Lottie?" one of the other girls asked sweetly.

Lottie poked miserably with a fork at her baked potato and cheese. Why hadn't she just pushed her way out of the huddle and sat somewhere else? Even sitting completely on her own would have been better than this. She would just have to ignore them. They couldn't actually do anything to her, after all.

"School food is awful, isn't it?" Zara said sympathetically. "It's got no flavour at all." She reached into her bag and pulled out a small packet. "This should help." She smiled, still looking completely sweet and friendly, and tipped the contents over Lottie's food.

Lottie started sneezing, again and again, her eyes burning. She wondered for half a second if Zara was a witch too, and had put a spell on her – weird things happening had tended to mean magic over the last few weeks – but it was just pepper.

She looked up at Zara, her eyes running with peppery tears, but she was glad. This she could deal with. She was furious, and it was far better to be angry than frightened and upset by mean whispering. She picked up her plate and tipped it upside down on top of Zara's. Then she fixed her dark eyes on Zara's round blue ones. Ariadne had taught her how strong the power of a stare could be. It was one of the things that made cats so spooky sometimes.

Zara looked quite disconcerted. Lottie didn't even have to look inside her mind to tell that she'd expected her to collapse in a heap and howl.

"Leave . . . me . . . alone," Lottie snarled, still fixing Zara with her glare, and she pushed her chair back with a shriek that made everyone in the hall turn round in surprise. Then she barged her way past Bethany and Amy, not being particularly careful who she kicked on the way.

The hall was noisy with clattering knives and forks and first-day-of-school chattering, but lots of people, especially the year sixes, were silent as they watched her go. Most of them eyed Zara's table thoughtfully as Lottie headed out of the door.

The teacher on lunch duty intercepted her at the door.

"Are you all right? It's . . . Lottie, isn't it? Do you need anything?" Clearly she'd noticed something was going on, but she wasn't sure what.

Lottie could feel six pairs of eyes burning into her back as Zara and her friends wondered what she'd say. She wasn't going to tell. On her first day, and make herself look like a real baby? No, they'd get away with it this time. At least she'd managed to ruin Zara's lunch too. She just smiled and said she was nipping to the loo. But as Lottie walked slowly down the corridor, trying to remember which way her classroom was, she felt her eyes filling with more tears, ones that she couldn't blame on the pepper. She had to survive at least a term of this, maybe even a whole year, and she was sick of it already.

Lottie arrived back at the shop feeling exhausted.

"Lottie's back! Lottie's back!" The mouse cages lining the walls of the shop were suddenly full of bouncing, squeaking little creatures. Lottie's favourites, the pink mice, were practically in hysterics with excitement.

"How was it, Lottie?" they chirruped enthusiastically. "We missed you! Tell us what it was like!"

Uncle Jack hurried in from the storeroom, looking hopeful. "Did you have a good day?"

Lottie summoned up a smile. She wished she could just drag herself up to her bedroom and lie down, preferably with her head under her pillow, but it wouldn't be fair. Besides, it was nice to be missed. At least someone liked her, she thought miserably.

Despite her brave stand against Zara and the others, Lottie felt really down. It was all very well pretending she couldn't care less, but it looked like she was going to have no friends at Netherbridge Hill, ever. By the time lunch had ended, Zara's lot had gone round every single girl in Lottie's class and made it very clear that they could and would make their lives a misery if they spoke so much as a word to that new girl, Lottie Grace. The other girls might not like Zara, but they knew her, after going all the way through the school with her. There was no way they were going to risk upsetting her for the sake of some new girl they'd never met.

No one had said a word to Lottie all afternoon, except for Mrs Laurence. And, strangely enough, Zara, who was still keeping up her sweetness-and-light act in front of the teacher.

An hour and a half of pretending she couldn't care less had left Lottie feeling limp. She was starving as well, having had nothing to eat since breakfast, which she hadn't felt like anyway.

"Let me just go and grab some raisins or something," she promised Uncle Jack and the mice. "Then I'll tell you everything."

There was a sudden scrabbling of claws and Sofie galloped down the stairs, her polished black nails clicking on the floorboards as she dashed in and flung herself into Lottie's arms. Lottie was so surprised she almost dropped her, and she did drop the bag of raisins. It showed how distracted Sofie was that she didn't immediately get down to wolf them up.

"Are you all right?" Lottie asked worriedly. Sofie was not a very cuddly dog, and she was usually extremely dignified. Leaping into someone's arms wasn't her style at all.

"Of course I am!" Sofie's French accent had intensified, like it always did when she was embarrassed or cross. She wriggled as though she hadn't wanted to be picked up at all, and jumped on to one of the kitchen chairs. "So, how was school?" she asked, trying not to sound too interested, and failing.

"Horrible," Lottie muttered, her shoulders tensing up. "I haven't had any lunch and I'm starving." She picked up the raisins that had fallen on the floor, and was heading for the bin when Sofie coughed meaningfully.

"The floor is very clean," the little dog said, eyeing the raisins hopefully.

Lottie grinned. Sofie's food obsession always made her laugh. "OK, then. I promised I'd tell the mice about school too; come and eat them in the shop."

They sat down behind the counter, and Lottie started to tell everyone what had happened. It was good to have a sympathetic audience, and they were already primed to despise Zara after the way she'd behaved to Tabitha. Neither Sofie nor the mice could stand cats on principle, but as the mice said, Tabitha wasn't that bad for a cat. Their reaction was gratifyingly furious. Even Horace the parrot hissed with disgust when Lottie got to the bit about the pepper, and Lottie hadn't thought Horace actually liked her very much.

Uncle Jack was looking horrified. He'd been worried about Lottie when Zara and the others picked on her over the holidays, and he'd been hoping that it wouldn't carry on at school. "Maybe I should go in and see your teacher," he murmured worriedly. "Nice woman, Mrs Laurence. She has a very intelligent bull terrier; I've always thought he could talk if he wanted to."

Lottie shook her head. "No. No thanks, Uncle Jack. Not yet, anyway. It would just make it worse." She sighed. "I'm going to go and relax upstairs for a bit, is that OK? You don't need anything doing?"

"Go, go!" Uncle Jack shooed her, flapping his hands, still looking worried. "We'll talk about it all later, when Danny gets back." He looked at his watch. "He should be here soon."

Lottie hauled herself up the stairs, Sofie trotting beside her. It was on days like this that she was really grateful to her mum for sending her regular packages full of yummy French chocolates. Sofie was starting to look distinctly plump round the ribs, though.

Strangely, Sofie didn't seem hungry today. She'd only had a few raisins downstairs, so Lottie stared at her worriedly. "Are you all right?" she asked. "Look, this is a violet cream, they're your favourite."

Sofie just grunted. She had her nose on her paws, and she looked extremely solemn. "Lottie, is it really that bad, this school?" she murmured.

Lottie stared at the chocolate box, remembering the awful afternoon, with no one talking to her – except Zara, who was either being sweet and helpful, or hissing whispered threats, depending on how close Mrs Laurence was. How was she ever supposed to concentrate on any work?

She shrugged miserably. "It was pretty horrible. Only Zara, though. Without her it would probably be all right."

"Oh." Sofie rested her nose on her paws again.

"Sofie, what's the matter? I mean, it's nice that you're sad for me, but normally you'd tell me to stop being so stupid and go and bite Zara, or something. Why are you so – down?"

Sofie sat up. Her ears and whiskers were drooping, and she looked deeply unhappy. "You are going to leave. . ." she whispered. "Your mother, she is missing you, and now you hate this school. She will come back and take you away, I think."

"Do you think she might?" Lottie asked eagerly. The idea had been hovering in the back of her mind all the way home.

Sofie nodded. "Perhaps. If you ask her." She turned

round and crawled on her tummy up to the other end of Lottie's bed, curling herself into a small, black ball. Her face was hidden, and Lottie had to strain her ears to hear Sofie whisper, "You are going to leave me behind, yes?"

Lottie gaped at her. "Of course not!" she said in a horrified voice. "I couldn't, Sofie, you know I couldn't. You're my familiar. It would be like leaving a part of me behind."

Sofie unrolled sufficiently for Lottie to see one gleaming black eye. "So you would take me with you? Back home? Back to your mother's house?"

Lottie stared at her, finally thinking this through. "Um, yes." Then she added, "But it's not a house, it's a flat." There was a slightly longer pause, while Sofie said nothing either, and then Lottie said quietly, "I'm not actually sure dogs are allowed."

"I thought not. And your mother, she does not love dogs, hmm?" Sofie's one visible eye was fixed on Lottie's face now, grimly demanding the truth.

Lottie shook her head. "Not really. . . She's more of a cat person, if anything," she admitted.

Sofie whispered a growl. "I thought as much. So, Lottie, you are still thinking we will go and live with your mother?"

Lottie stared at her hands. School was awful, a disaster, completely unbearable. Or so she had thought. Her one desire had been to escape. Now

Sofie had forced her to think about the real alternative – going back home. It was what Lottie had longed for, argued for, fought for, at the beginning of her stay. But how could she do it now? Now, when she was used to brushing her teeth in the mornings with two pink mice dangling upside down in front of the mirror and arguing about who had the silkiest fur? When she was learning the deepest secrets of a family she'd never known? When she ate breakfast discussing her magical homework with a small, black, coffee-drinking dog? When that same dog was her closest friend, when they were two halves of a magical whole, when going home would mean leaving her for ever?

Lottie took a deep breath, images whirling through her mind. "No, I see it now," she said slowly. "I have to stay. I just have to. I'll manage with school. And I don't know how we'll do it when Mum does want me back, but I can't leave you, Sofie. This is my home now."

3

Lottie walked to school slowly the next day. Partly because she really didn't want to get there, but also because the walk gave her some time to think, away from the shop. Sofie had given her a huge shock. Even though she loved the shop, Lottie had assumed that if a miracle happened, and her mother gave up the Paris job and came home to their old flat, she would be delighted to go back to everything the way it had been before. Now it was as though Sofie had pulled a rug from under her feet – Lottie felt wobbly all over.

It wasn't just leaving Sofie behind (because the little dachshund was right, Lottie really couldn't see her mum ever having a dog in the flat), it was the shop too. Lottie felt part of something now, something special. And how could she give up on her training with Ariadne? Even though she came home from quite a few of the lessons feeling useless, Lottie never wished she didn't have magic in her blood.

When Uncle Jack had fretted at her over supper last night, suggesting again that he went to talk to someone at the school, Lottie had noted the worried furrows between Sofie's ears. Sofie was very carefully digging the bits of bacon out of her pasta and pretending not to care about anything else, but clearly she was anxious.

Lottie smiled at Uncle Jack. "It'll be fine," she said, with a lot more confidence than she really felt. "It's just that I'm the only new girl. They'll get used to me soon." She crossed all her fingers under the table as she said it, and saw the wrinkles smooth away from Sofie's velvety fur.

Danny looked at her thoughtfully. Lottie realized he could see her hands and uncrossed them quickly, but surprisingly he didn't tease her about it. He almost looked sympathetic, and Lottie suddenly wondered how his first day had been. He'd got back a little while after Lottie, and she had a horrible feeling that Uncle Jack had been too worried about her to make a big thing of Danny's first day at secondary school. She felt guilty. "What's your school like?" she asked him.

Uncle Jack looked guilty too; she'd been right. "Danny, I'm sorry, I haven't asked!" he said, sounding horrified. "I was on the phone to the seed people when you got back – the last batch of the special sunflower seed actually exploded, you know, it's just not good enough – and then you disappeared up to your room so fast. . ." He trailed off, obviously feeling as though he was making excuses.

"It's school," Danny muttered, glaring at Lottie. "What more do you want me to say?" He didn't seem grateful for the attention at all. In fact, he obviously wanted to avoid attention entirely, Lottie thought, watching with professional interest as her cousin went slightly misty around the edges. He wasn't actually trying to disappear, just wanting them to forget about him for a bit. On people without magic, it would definitely have worked.

"We can all still see you," Sofie said, watching him with her head on one side.

Danny sighed. "If you must know, it was grim, all right? None of my mates are in my class, and I kept getting lost. And I don't want to talk about it any more." He stuffed a forkful of Uncle Jack's special curried cauliflower into his mouth by accident in his hurry not to be able to answer any more questions, and looked disgusted.

No one had quite known what to say, Lottie thought to herself as she wandered along. They were all so used to Danny being cool and self-sufficient and confident and just generally sorted, that they stared at him in shock when he admitted things hadn't gone perfectly.

"Maybe it'll be better tomorrow?" Uncle Jack said, a bit feebly.

Danny just glared at him, and Uncle Jack got up to clear the plates in a hurry. "Chocolate cake!" he announced, sounding as though he felt chocolate cake should cure anything. Danny and Lottie exchanged glances. Sometimes, Lottie thought, Uncle Jack just didn't want to think about difficult things. Maybe he and her dad were similar in that way too? They had looked very alike, going by the photos. Mum had said that Dad wasn't very good at being responsible, and maybe Uncle Jack was the same.

Lottie walked into the school playground, and watched everyone immediately take in a sharp breath. They all knew. No one was going to talk to her; Zara had frightened them all off. She might just about be able to join in with the reception babies if she didn't tell them her name, but that was it. Quick huddles were formed as everyone tried to look busy in case Lottie attempted to talk to them.

Lottie stared firmly straight ahead and marched determinedly through the playground to a bench. She grinned to herself as the two girls sitting on it, who were both in her class, scurried away before they could be accused of fraternizing with the enemy. It was almost funny, in a painful sort of way. She sat down, and got out the homework diary she'd been given the day before. They hadn't been given any homework, but she needed to pretend to be busy with *something*.

"You're a bit keen, aren't you?" someone said, thumping down beside her, and Lottie looked up in shock. She was just about to warn this pretty, freckly, red-haired girl that she wasn't supposed to talk to her, when she realized that Zara had even got *her* thinking she was an exile. She shook her head. Wow. It was amazing what a whispering campaign could do after only a day.

She grinned at the other girl. "You weren't here yesterday, were you?" she asked thoughtfully.

The red-haired girl's freckles were hidden by a blush. "Um, no. . ." She looked down at her hands, and then nibbled one of her nails. "My mum got the dates mixed up, if you must know. She's busy," she added defensively. "Working."

Lottie smiled sympathetically. "Mine too. She's gone to Paris for work, and left me in Netherbridge."

"Oh well, that beats mine, she's only in the garden. But she might as well be in Paris. Once she gets started, you can't get her out again." But the red-haired girl sounded relieved to have met someone else whose mother wasn't perfect either.

"Is she a gardener?" Lottie asked interestedly.

"Nooo!" The red-haired girl had a great laugh; just listening to her giggling made Lottie feel much better. "She's an artist. She has a studio out there. She makes weird things out of wire and beads and bits of stuff she finds in the garden. Then she sells them for loads of money, which is excellent, but she's a bit useless on making the tea and remembering when term starts, that kind of thing. I'm Ruby Geddis. Don't say anything about rubies and my hair, please, I've heard it all."

Lottie nodded eagerly. "I'm Lottie Grace. I'm living with my uncle at the pet shop in town. Do you live in Netherbridge? Or do you have to come in from one of the villages?"

"Oh no, we live just at the edge of the town. By the river. I've not been here most of the summer, though; we went on a really boring 'holiday' that was actually my mum visiting loads of galleries that sell her stuff, and my dad disappearing into antique shops. It was the worst ever. I'm actually glad to be back at school."

Ruby really did look quite happy, and Lottie felt guilty. What if she minded about Zara and the others not talking to her? It wasn't fair not to warn her. "Um, there's something I ought to tell you," she said reluctantly.

Ruby was giving her an interested look when they both suddenly realized that someone else had arrived. Several someone elses, actually. Zara was standing there with her arms folded, and her friends were lined up behind her looking like some sort of Mafia gang.

"Because you weren't here yesterday, Ruby Geddis, we're willing to let you off. But you have to stop talking to her *now*," Zara said, sternly.

Ruby looked confused. "What?" she asked.

Zara clicked her tongue irritably. "Nobody is talking to her!" she snapped.

"I am," Ruby said earnestly, smiling. Lottie couldn't tell if she really didn't understand Zara or she was being difficult for the fun of it, but there was a glint in her eye that suggested she knew exactly what she was doing.

"Well, you shouldn't be!" Clearly Ruby knew how to get to Zara; she was looking really annoyed, digging her nails into the palms of her hands, and practically hissing.

Ruby just gazed back at her innocently. "Why?"

"Because we said so," Zara said, sounding triumphant – after all, no one would dare go against her. They knew what she could do. "Anyone who talks to her *goes on our list. . .*"

"Oh." Ruby nodded as though she understood, and Lottie felt tears burn behind her eyes. Ruby had seemed so nice, and for a few minutes she'd forgotten about how horrible school was going to be. Now it was ruined again. She stared at her homework diary, willing the tears back.

A hand tapped her on the shoulder. "Want to come for a walk, Lottie?" Ruby suggested, ignoring the sharp intake of breath from Zara and her chorus.

"But. . ." Lottie glanced quickly at Zara, and then away again, for the expression on her face was truly scary. She looked murderous.

Ruby grinned. "That's OK. I've been trying to get Zara not to speak to me for years. I wish you'd come along before. Did anyone show you our school garden yet? Come and see." And she got up and strolled off. Zara was left staring after her, and her china-pretty face had cracked, like a mask.

Lottie grabbed her stuff and ran. In theory, she knew that Zara couldn't do anything to her, but actually, the gang terrified her. She scurried after Ruby, wishing she could be as brave – except Ruby didn't look as though she was *being* brave; she just didn't seem to care.

Ruby smiled at her over her shoulder. "So what did you do to get on the wrong side of Zara Martin on your first day?" she enquired. "That was fast work."

Lottie shook her head. "It was in the holidays," she explained. "They were having a go at me about my mum. . ." She thought quickly, trying to remember a version of the story that was safe to tell, one that didn't involve being given directions by a talking dog. "It was really embarrassing; my cousin Danny came along, and he had to sort of rescue me."

"Oh, are you Danny Grace's cousin? You look a teensy bit like him, I suppose. Everyone thought he was the cutest boy in the school, you know." Ruby was staring at her, clearly trying to see the resemblance.

Lottie made a disgusted face, and Ruby giggled.

"Not when you do that." Then she looked serious, or as serious as she seemed to get. "Watch out for Zara, Lottie," she said, frowning. "She can be really, really mean. My friend Lucy, when we were year four, Zara made her so miserable she left. She actually had to go to boarding school just to get away from her. And Zara never, ever gets caught. She managed to make the school think it was Lucy bullying *her*."

Lottie nodded. She could see that, all too easily. She resolved to watch her back. But as she listened to Ruby chattily pointing out year six's garden patch, and wondering what they might plant in it this year, Lottie thought how nice it was that now maybe someone else was watching out for her too.

4

The next day Lottie nipped home from school to fetch Sofie, and they went over to Ariadne's flat for some witch training. Lottie had loads of homework already, and she was really hoping that Ariadne wouldn't give her stuff to take home as well. She leaned hard on Ariadne's doorbell, and there was a chorus of yowls from inside. Sofie barked back. Lottie didn't know what she was saying, but it sounded rude.

Shadow and Tabitha, Ariadne's two cat familiars, were twining themselves possessively round her ankles as she opened the door. They fluffed up their tails when they saw Sofie. Although she and the cats knew each other perfectly well, and met most days, they still pretended to dislike each other, and always exchanged rude remarks for the sake of it.

They sat down at the table in Ariadne's shining white and silver kitchen, and Ariadne gave Lottie a serious look round her coffee mug. "You look exhausted," she said. "Of course, I haven't seen you since school started. Is it awful?"

Lottie shrugged. "Ish. Term started on Wednesday so at least I've only had three days of it this first week. I've got the weekend to recover now." She sighed. "The first day was really bad, but then I met a girl called Ruby, and she's actually nice. She's the only person who's talking to me, though."

"Why?" Tabitha, like Shadow, had a beautiful voice – low, purring and almost hypnotic.

Lottie glanced at Ariadne. She didn't want to upset Tabitha by telling her about Zara. It was only a few weeks since Lottie and Sofie had found Zara's gang teasing poor, half-starved Tabitha, and rescued her. But Tabitha was Ariadne's familiar now, and these days she missed very little that concerned her mistress, for their thoughts were so closely linked. "What is it, Lottie?" she purred gently.

Lottie felt the sweetness of Tabitha's purr catching at the corners of her mind. "Don't!" she said sharply. "I was going to tell you, I just didn't want to make you upset. You don't need to fish it out for yourself."

Tabitha flowed across the table from her position on Ariadne's left (Shadow still sat to her right, as her oldest cat) and rubbed her chin against the side of Lottie's face. Sofie watched her suspiciously. "I'm sorry. But you shouldn't keep secrets, Lottie," Tabitha added reproachfully. "Why did you look at us like that?"

Sofie sat up straighter on Lottie's lap. "It's Zara. Lottie's trying to be tactful by not telling you. She hasn't realized yet that there's no point trying to be polite round a nosy bunch of cats."

Tabitha hissed, but not at Sofie. The memory of Zara was clear and strong. It was almost as though a picture of her appeared in the air above the table, with a smaller, thinner, sadder Tabitha cowering at her feet.

"Sssshhh, ssshhh!" Ariadne had gone pale as Tabitha's fear ran through her and Shadow. She gathered Tabitha into her arms, and Shadow leaned against them both, his milky, near-blind eyes worried, his breath wheezing slightly.

"No one will hurt you, little one," Shadow hissed. "You're safe here."

Even Sofie yapped sharply, as though the memory hurt her too. "Silly little cat!" she snapped. "As if we'd let her get to you again." And she nudged Lottie's arm firmly with her nose, to remind her that that went for her too.

Lottie shook herself. Tabitha's memory picture had brought horrible Zara into the lovely, quiet flat, where she felt so safe. Or at least, where she knew there were people who cared for her. Lottie had begun to realize that magic wasn't always safe – she was sure something bad had happened to her dad because of it – but sometimes, that was what made it so special.

"She really has you scared," Shadow said thoughtfully. "I can smell it on you. What does she do to you, this girl?"

Lottie flushed. It was embarrassing to admit how much Zara upset her. Especially to Shadow, as the elderly cat wasn't the most sympathetic listener – except to Tabitha, whom he adored.

For once, Shadow surprised her. "Tell us, Lottie dear. We can't help you if you keep it hidden. We know how hard it is for you to be in a new place yet again. Even though we ourselves have forgotten what it is to be young and frightened, Ariadne and I have Tabitha's memories to draw on now. We've seen Zara in her mind, and we know how cruel she is. You've no need to feel ashamed." He fixed his opal eyes on Lottie. She knew he could hardly see her, but if she let him, the magic could see everything, even through worn-out eyes.

Did she trust them enough?

Lottie thought for a second. When she saw the vision of Zara, Lottie had been horrified partly because it had stolen into a place where she was only loved – even by grumpy Shadow. She felt Sofie in her mind, a soft brown velvet presence telling her to let them in.

Lottie smiled at her. How had Sofie ever thought she could leave her behind? She sighed, and relaxed, and melted the icy hold she had around her mind.

Ariadne let out a long sighing breath, sank her chin on her hands and gazed at Lottie.

Lottie was never sure how long they sat. It felt like days, and yet only seconds might have passed. She felt warm all over, and comforted, as though she'd been cold for a very long time, and someone had wrapped a furry blanket around her. Yes, definitely furry. Ariadne's mind felt clear and jade-green, the colour of a beautiful stone bracelet of her mother's that Lottie was allowed to borrow occasionally. But the two cats had rushed through her mind in a coiling mass of black and brown and grey softness. It struck Lottie that even though she thought fur coats were cruel, she could see why people had once worn them, for there was nothing so comforting as fur.

"Better *on* than off, Lottie," Tabitha mewed, and Lottie blinked.

"Oh! I forgot you were still listening! Sorry, it was just a silly thought. It felt like you'd wrapped a fur coat round me inside. It's lovely," she finished lamely, unable to describe it.

Sofie shuddered her whiskers. "I cannot believe I just had a cat in my head," she muttered. "A cat!"

"Two cats." Shadow let out a wheezy chuckle. "Get used to it, little dog."

Ariadne ignored their bickering. "You've had those barriers up a long time, Lottie. I wonder if it's to do with living away from magic? You felt you had to keep it controlled."

"Oh!" Lottie sat up straight, the pleasant furry weariness slipping away. "I forgot, I meant to ask you, Ariadne. When Mum was here, she said that once I broke a cup in the old tea shop that used to be where Valentin's is now. She said she couldn't see how I'd done it, because she didn't think I was anywhere near. Could that have been magic? Baby magic somehow? I think I was only about two."

Ariadne nodded. "Probably. You were round magic all the time then; your own magic would have wanted to reach out to it – like you as a toddler, wanting to play. But then when your mum took you away, your magic had nothing to learn from. And your mum would have been so sad. That would have kept the magic muffled too."

Lottie nodded. It sounded awful, her magic surrounded and suffocated by sadness. She was more glad every day that she'd come back to Netherbridge. And she was growing more and more certain that she had to stay – she couldn't leave the world of magic now.

"Your mother is still very much on your mind, Lottie," Ariadne said. "Everything seems to lead back to her. Her visit didn't sort things out, did it?"

Lottie frowned. "It did and it didn't," she admitted eventually. "It was wonderful to see her, and I'm not angry with her any more. I learned a lot when we saw her in Paris, and we talked when she was here. I feel like I know her a lot better, and I understand why she does things. Why she's the way she is, I suppose. But – well, there are still problems." Lottie took a deep breath. It felt good to talk about all of this, even though it was difficult. "It's so hard to know that I can never tell her about all of this. Something so important and special, and I can never share it with her." She looked at Sofie, whose dark-brown eyes were fixed worriedly on hers. "And I'm scared about what's going to happen to me. To us. I mean, this can't last for ever, can it? Her Paris job was meant to be a short placement, even though it's been extended once. Sooner or later, she's going to come back, and she'll want *me* back." Lottie was fighting tears away, and Sofie was pressing her head hard against her tummy. Lottie could hear her thinking fiercely, *I will never let you go, never!* It was so unlike her proud, sophisticated, independent Sofie that it made Lottie want to giggle, even then.

She held Sofie close, trying to calm them both. "I thought that was what I wanted, especially when school was so bad the first day, but I hadn't really been thinking about it. It was more as though I had it written down in my mind, and it was something I just – knew. Well, now I know that it was wrong. I can't go back. And I'm going to have to tell her that, and honestly I don't know how I can. She's lost my dad, and now she's got to lose me too?"

No one said anything. There was nothing to say – no easy answer. Ariadne just gazed sadly at her, and Tabitha climbed into Lottie's lap and put her face against Sofie's. Sofie, for once, didn't complain, even when Tabitha affectionately licked her nose.

"We will help," Shadow said at last. "We cannot say how, but when the time comes, we will help. You will not have to do this alone. Remember that." He nodded firmly. "And the same goes for this Zara creature. Do not let her make you forget you have friends. That is what she does; she makes you feel alone and friendless, which you are not."

Ariadne smiled. "Yes, I caught a glimpse of Ruby in your mind, Lottie. She could be another good friend."

Lottie smiled. She thought so too. "But then that's another problem, isn't it?" she said suddenly. "What do I tell her about the shop? Danny never even invites any of his mates round, because he's too embarrassed, or perhaps he's scared that they'll find out the secret. I'd like Ruby to come over, but maybe it's too dangerous."

Ariadne shook her head firmly. "No. Danny's wrong, Lottie. He's far too worried about his image, and it's partly living above a messy, weird old shop that he wants to hide, not even the magic. I tried to talk to him about school when I popped in yesterday, while you were out with Sofie. He seems unhappy. I was hoping this new school would be a good change for him, that he could be more himself, but he was more closed off than ever. You can't hide yourself away, Lottie. If Ruby is the kind of person she seems to be, then she won't care that the shop is a little – strange." Ariadne paused thoughtfully. "I *would* warn those chatty mice, though," she added.

5

The shop seemed a blissful haven to Lottie that weekend, more so than ever. When she got back from Ariadne's on Friday afternoon, even the musty, rather mousey smell made her feel better. As always, there was a tiny silence as she opened the door, as the animals inside worked out if they could safely talk in front of who was coming in; then they went on chattering.

"Look what we can do, Lottie!" chirruped two of the pink mice.

Lottie stood on tiptoe to see their cage, and watched anxiously as one climbed on to the other's shoulders. They wobbled wildly for thirty seconds and then fell over.

"What did you do that for?" squeaked one.

"Me! It was you, swaying about like that. Can't you just learn to stand still?" the other snapped back. "I could have broken something. I'm sure I've sprained my tail as it is. Lottie, look, it didn't bend like that before, did it?" The mouse poked his tail through the cage bars and peered down at her anxiously.

"It is just the same as it always is," Sofie snapped. "A mouse tail. Now go away, we are busy." And she pranced past the mouse cages with her nose in the air.

Lottie gave the mice an apologetic look. "She's tired. We had a hard time at Ariadne's. Sorry. I think your tail looks beautiful."

"I heard that!" Sofie yapped. "I am not tired in the slightest."

The mouse sniffed in a dramatic sort of way, but seemed comforted. As Lottie went to find Uncle Jack in the kitchen, she heard him proudly telling the others: "Beautiful! Did you hear her? She said it's beautiful. *My* tail. That's what Lottie said."

Danny was home already, leaning on the counter with his chin on his hands, and occasionally passing a sunflower seeds to Septimus, the black rat, who was lounging next to him. Lottie wasn't sure she'd ever actually seen Septimus upright. He was more of a horizontal rat.

"Hi Danny," Lottie said, feeling cheerful at the thought of no school, and no Zara, for two whole days.

Danny grunted something.

Septimus grinned at her, showing enormous yellowish teeth. "Hello Lottie. I wouldn't bother, he's in a filthy temper. I've almost bitten him twice and he's only been home half an hour."

"Oh." Lottie thought for a minute. "Did you have

to stay after school, then?" she asked Danny. "I thought you'd have been home ages ago; it felt like we were at Ariadne's for hours."

"Got a detention yesterday," Danny muttered. "An hour after school, on a Friday. It's cruelty to children."

Lottie gaped at him. "You got a detention? On your second day?"

Danny nodded. "And don't you dare tell Dad."

Septimus chuckled. "We had to resort to forgery, Lottie." He showed her the tip of his tail, which was stained inky-black. "Luckily, I can do a very passable imitation of your uncle's signature for the detention slip. Hence the sunflower seeds. He owes me."

"What did you *do*?" Lottie asked, curiously.

Danny sighed. He looked really miserable. "Nothing," he said, looking up at her, his eyes tired. "That's what makes it really annoying. It wasn't me. A load of guys in my class chucked a ball through a window and smashed it. When they got dragged in to see the head, they said I'd kicked it."

"But didn't you say it wasn't you?" Lottie asked indignantly.

Danny shrugged. "They all swore blind it was, Lottie." He rubbed his hands over his face wearily. "And these are the ones everyone in my class likes. Everyone wants to be in with them. If I landed them in it, the whole class would hate me. As it is –" he looked suddenly hopeful – "maybe now I've taken the blame for the window, they'll let me hang around with them too."

Lottie looked at him doubtfully. Why did he want to hang around with such a load of losers? But she didn't say it. She didn't think Danny needed someone arguing with him right now.

But Septimus was watching her through narrowed eyes, and he gave her a tiny nod, which Lottie took to mean he thought the same. Septimus loved Danny. If Danny bothered to use his magic, Lottie was sure that Septimus would be his familiar, although possibly it would involve too much effort.

"Are you doing much this weekend?" Lottie asked. Danny was always out with his mates.

Danny shrugged, looking even more depressed. "Dunno. Most of my friends from Netherbridge Hill are in the other year seven classes. They've all got stuff planned, and I feel really stupid asking if I can come too. Like I should have things to do with my own lot."

Lottie gave a sympathetic nod. "I bet they wouldn't mind," she suggested cautiously.

Danny gave her a look of dislike. "I'm not going crawling to them," he snapped.

Septimus rolled his eyes at Lottie. *Don't bother*, his expression said, quite clearly.

Sofie, who'd clambered up the step stool to rest her paws on the counter too, glared at Danny. "You are very bad-tempered today, my little cabbage," she observed disapprovingly.

Danny glared back. "Shut up, Sofie," he snarled. He shoved his stool away from the counter with a screech, and stomped off upstairs.

Sofie fluttered her eyelashes at Lottie and Septimus. "Did I say something wrong?" she asked innocently.

Danny seemed to have cheered up a bit the next morning. He was quiet at breakfast, but at least he wasn't scowling. He ploughed his way through a huge mound of toast, staring into the distance and not seeing anyone.

"What's the matter with him?" Lottie asked Sofie, who was delicately sipping a very strong black coffee and shuddering. She was not a morning dog.

Sofie wrinkled her nose. "I do not know. But if he does not stop eating toast, it will be indigestion."

Just then, Danny seemed to come back to life. He stared at Lottie, his dark eyes fixing her so powerfully that Lottie wondered why on earth he was not bothering to use his magic. It was obvious that he would be amazingly good at it.

Perhaps Danny was thinking along the same lines. "Ariadne's teaching you magic, isn't she?" he asked, as if they were already in the middle of a conversation.

Lottie gave him a surprised look. "Yes. Except I never feel as though I'm learning very much."

Sofie shook her head decidedly. "No, Lottie. You do not realize. It is all, what is the word, *seeping* in. Slowly," she admitted. "But we will get there. It does not happen overnight."

Lottie looked at her hopefully. This was the most anyone had ever said about her magic developing. Up until now, Sofie had just told her to work harder.

Danny waved a hand irritably. "So I could ask her some stuff, maybe?"

"Of course. . ." Lottie said slowly. A sudden pinprick of fear grew in her chest. What if Ariadne would rather teach Danny, who would probably learn really quickly and be a fantastic pupil?

"Excellent." Danny leaped up from the table and thundered up the stairs, still holding a piece of toast.

Sofie scratched at her arm with her shiny black claws, and Lottie jumped.

"No," Sofie said firmly.

Lottie gave her a confused look, and Sofie sighed in that particularly French way she had that meant Lottie was doing something stupid. "Lott-ee, we are bonded," she said, as though talking to a very small and very dim child. "I can see what you are thinking. No. Ariadne will not do that. She loves Danny, but I do not think she could teach him. They would murder each other." She sipped her coffee thoughtfully.

49

"Besides, he does not want lessons, Lottie. Did you not hear him? He wants to ask her things, to have answers. He would not just sit still and be taught."

Lottie felt a bit better. But, she couldn't help worrying that Danny would be brilliant, and Ariadne would wish she was teaching him instead. . .

Danny lost no time. As soon as Ariadne arrived at the shop later that morning, he sweetly offered to make her a cup of coffee, and started to ask tricky questions.

Uncle Jack listened delightedly. It had only taken a few weeks of Lottie living at the shop to realize that he desperately wanted Danny to use his talents. He would hint at it every so often, but he'd been trying not to put any pressure on, knowing how stubborn Danny was. Now he hovered round the kitchen door, ignoring several customers and smiling to himself. He even dug out a tin of rather good chocolate biscuits that he'd been hoarding at the back of a cupboard.

Ariadne also seemed delighted that Danny was interested. Lottie wondered miserably if it was jealousy that made her the only person who found Danny's sudden interest in using his magic suspicious. Was she really that mean? she thought to herself guiltily.

But Sofie peered round the kitchen door, and then

gave her a knowing look. "He is up to something, that one," she said decisively. "We must keep an eye on him." She nodded to herself. Then she looked round with interest as the shop bell jangled. "Look, a new customer," she hissed.

Lottie turned round, smiling, ready to serve the new arrival. Uncle Jack was still eavesdropping on Danny, who was picking Ariadne's brains about glamours, a complicated branch of spellcraft that made people see things that weren't really there.

The customer was clearly magical, but strangely, the animals hadn't launched into their usual chatty commentary, even though she obviously knew what they were. Instead there was a nervous hush, broken by the odd whisper. The only noise, besides the low hum of voices from the kitchen, was Horace grumpily spitting out sunflower-seed shells. He seemed to be doing it with extra force today, and Lottie gave him a surprised look. He stared back, his eyes watchful and grim.

Lottie began to feel worried.

The tall, beautiful woman in the red dress gave Lottie a charming smile. If she hadn't been warned by the animals' nervousness, Lottie would have fallen for it straight away. As it was, she smiled cautiously back, and slammed up every guard round her mind that Ariadne had managed to teach her.

The woman – the witch – looked slightly taken

aback. Lottie guessed that trying to use the power on her had felt a bit like running into a brick wall. Her smile became rather steely.

"I'm looking for some mice," she said, very gently. "I've been told you have some rather special ones. Perhaps you could show me?"

Lottie didn't move. Suddenly, she couldn't bear to sell anything to this woman. Not even mouse food. Everything about her was *wrong*. Lottie gulped.

Sofie growled softly behind her. Her velvety voice was sharp and urgent in Lottie's head. *Do not let her take any of our animals! She wants them for bad things. . .* Then she turned back towards the kitchen and seized Uncle Jack's trouser leg in her teeth. "Come!" she snapped.

Uncle Jack started and gazed vaguely down at her. Sofie yapped sharply, and he shook himself, at last noticing the witch in red. His face hardened suddenly, as though the bones were showing through the skin. Lottie had never been afraid of Uncle Jack, even though she knew he must be able to work very strong magic, but he looked frightening now. He moved forward into the shop and smiled politely at the red-dressed woman. "Can I help you?" he asked coldly.

She smiled. "As I was explaining to your *little girl* –" her emphasis was terrifying – "I am looking for some mice."

Lottie looked up at the mouse cages protectively.

She couldn't help it. But she had to look carefully before she could see any of them. The mice were hidden, and silent for once, tucked under their bedding, behind their toys. One of the pink mice was lying flat on his cage floor with his tail over his eyes, obviously hoping that if he couldn't see the witch, she couldn't see him. It wasn't working.

"I know you're there, my dears," the witch said, in a low, humming voice. "Come out and say hello. . ."

Reluctantly, moving like puppets, the mice reappeared, but Uncle Jack snapped out his hand. "Not in my shop, if you please!" he said sharply, and the mice scuttled back to their hiding places, their spell-bonds broken.

The witch stared back at him. "How very unwise," she commented, in a voice like ice. "Do I take it that your mice are not for sale?"

"I'm afraid we have a strange shortage of mice today," Uncle Jack replied, his voice still relentlessly controlled. He waved a hand at the cages, with the mice all well-hidden. "As you can see – no mice seem to be available."

There was an audible sigh of relief, and Lottie saw a few tails twitch out of hiding places.

The witch gave one last considering look around the shop, and then walked out, smiling. She even closed the door quietly.

Lottie let out a shaking breath. She hadn't realized

she'd forgotten to breathe. She'd been expecting the witch to do something awful.

Uncle Jack sagged on to the stool behind the counter, and reached into his emergency boiled-sweet drawer.

Danny popped out from the kitchen; clearly he and Ariadne had been eavesdropping. She was still sitting at the table, looking pale. "Who was that, Dad?" Danny asked curiously.

"Someone you don't want to know," Uncle Jack muttered. "Are you all right, Lottie? She didn't hurt you?"

Lottie shook her head. She could still feel traces of the witch's mind lingering in her own. "No. She did try to enchant me, though, like she did with the mice. It's her smile, I think. She was *horrible*."

"Has she gone?" It was a squeaky, frightened whisper. One of the pink mice was holding the cage bars with trembling paws. All the others were still hidden, their bedding heaving with their panicky breaths.

"Yes, yes, it's all right, I promise. You can all come out." Trembling whiskers started to appear in the cages, and a pink nose here and there. Uncle Jack reached back into his emergency drawer and brought out a small black bottle. "Danny, get your mother's china thimble collection," he said, pulling the stopper out of the top. A rich, golden, buttery smell filled the shop, and Lottie was sure she could see rose-pink smoke pouring out of the bottle.

"What's that?" she asked, almost forgetting about the witch.

"Mouse brandy," Uncle Jack explained, taking the tiny china thimbles that Danny had handed him. "It's made from rose-hips. For absolute emergencies only."

Suddenly the mice seemed to make a remarkable recovery. They popped out of their cages (Uncle Jack didn't believe in locking them in; they stayed in the cages most of the time only because they had comfy bedding and lots of food) and lined up along the shelves, each trying to look as faint and desperate and in need of reviving as possible.

Uncle Jack only allowed them a tiny sip each, although half of the pink mice managed to get a sneaky second helping by running round to the back of the queue. Then they had to be helped back into their cage, hiccupping and trying to remember the words to "Three Blind Mice".

"Really, Uncle Jack, who *was* that?" Lottie asked, as she washed out the china thimbles at the kitchen sink, and Uncle Jack made tea for everyone.

Uncle Jack and Ariadne exchanged glances. "She was an enchantress," Ariadne said. "A bad witch, I suppose, if you want to call it that. No different from me—"

"She was a lot different from you," Lottie exclaimed indignantly. "You're not like that at all!"

"But I could be, Lottie, don't you see?" Ariadne's voice was tired. "It's all about the choices you make. And sometimes it can be very hard to know the right way to go."

"She's gone the wrong way, then?" Lottie asked, feeling cold inside.

"How?" Danny looked fascinated.

"Who knows?" Ariadne shrugged. Then she put her face in her hands, and her shoulders shook slightly. Tabitha and Shadow leaned against her protectively, purring love and reassurance. She whispered between her fingers, and the others had to strain to hear. "We all felt her – the coldness of her. I don't know why she's like that. . . I shouldn't think there's anyone left alive to tell you."

6

Ariadne's reaction to the enchantress in the shop shocked even Danny. But he kept returning to the subject, asking niggling little questions, until at last Ariadne went home early, after Shadow had snapped at Danny to mind his mouth or he'd get it well and truly clawed.

Danny didn't seem too daunted, even though Uncle Jack made him apologize. He was thoughtful all through dinner, and then when Lottie was instant messaging her old friends from home, Rachel and Hannah, he kept hanging around asking her about it too. It made it very difficult trying to have a normal chat online with people who had no idea about enchantresses, and would have laughed if Lottie had told them what her new life was like.

"But what do you think she *did*?" he wondered aloud.

Lottie got the feeling he was just using her as someone to talk at; he didn't really expect her to answer. She shrugged irritably, trying to type.

"It can't really have been *that* bad; I reckon Ariadne was probably overreacting. She's so fussy about stuff like that."

This time Lottie turned round and stared at him, her eyes narrowed. "Overreacting? Are you out of your mind? She was practically being sick on the floor!"

"Lott-ie, ugh!" Sofie complained from the armchair where she was curled, listening. "That is most disgusting!"

When Lottie went to bed, Danny was sprawled over the armchair, staring at the ceiling and scribbling occasional notes on a crumpled piece of paper.

Lottie lay in bed worrying about him, with Sofie snuggled under her arm. About ten minutes after Lottie had turned the light off, Sofie sat up. "What is it?" she snapped. "You are wriggling. I do not like it when you wriggle. I was almost asleep and then you wriggled on me. What is the matter?"

Lottie sat up too. "I'm worried about Danny. Don't you think he was being a bit suspicious earlier? He kept on and on about that enchantress. He just seemed way too interested in that sort of magic. You know, the wrong kind."

"Probably." Lottie felt Sofie shrug. "But what is he going to do? He is just a *boy*, Lottie. He is maybe thinking he will have some fun, do something a bit wicked. So? He gets his fingers burned, maybe." Sofie sniffed. "It might do him good. He is far too conceited, that one."

Lottie lay on her back, staring thoughtfully into the darkness. Maybe Sofie was right. Still, she couldn't help feeling troubled. Ariadne had told her how difficult it was to draw a line between "good" and "evil". That sometimes they could be the same thing, and it depended on who you were, and why you wanted to do things. It sounded as though it was awfully easy to start something that got out of control. But then, if there was anything they ought to worry about with Danny, Uncle Jack and Ariadne would have noticed. Wouldn't they?

When she got to school on Monday, Lottie looked around anxiously for Ruby. Then she realized what she was doing, and tried to make herself relax. Just because Ruby had been nice, it didn't necessarily mean she wanted to be best friends or anything. Lottie didn't want to come over as desperate. She sat on one of the benches, avoiding evil glares from a couple of Zara's friends, and tried to concentrate on a list of herbs that Ariadne had given her to learn. It was actually quite interesting, with all the different things that the herbs were good for, and the best ways to mix them. Lottie was grinning to herself over a note in Ariadne's spiky writing that it was nonsense that picking herbs by moonlight made any difference, except that you ended up picking the wrong ones because it was dark, when someone snatched the list.

Lottie gasped and jumped up to grab it back. Why had she been so stupid?! She should never have brought it to school. If anyone else read it, they would think she was a complete weirdo.

"Hey, give that back!" Ruby had just walked into the playground and seen what had happened.

Zara had jumped on to the bench and was looking at the list. A couple of her friends – Lottie still hadn't worked out their names; they all seemed to merge into one – were jostling Lottie to stop her climbing up too.

Zara turned the piece of paper over and looked down at Lottie in disgust. "There's nothing on it," she said disappointedly. She'd obviously been hoping for something embarrassing; maybe a letter, or something precious she could torture Lottie by stealing.

Lottie stared at the paper, her heart thudding painfully, not sure if she was relieved or terrified. Ariadne must have put some sort of charm on it! She hadn't said, but Zara was right, the paper was blank. The list of herbs had vanished. Was it written only for Lottie to read?

"What were you doing, staring at a blank piece of paper?" Zara jeered, waving it at her. "Writing poetry?" She giggled nastily, and her mates all sneered at Lottie.

Then Ruby squeezed behind the bench, grabbed a handful of Zara's hair, and yanked. Zara howled, and Lottie shot forward and seized the list.

Ruby bolted out from behind the bench and yelled, "Run!" and they raced away, giggling hysterically. They ran round the school building, and Ruby showed Lottie a dry, dusty, useful hiding place under the fire escape.

"Not that I like hiding from Zara," she pointed out defensively; then she shrugged and admitted, "But sometimes it's just easier."

Lottie gave her an embarrassed grin. "It's tiring having to not care all the time," she agreed. She realized that she was still holding the list, and stuffed it into her pocket, her face flushing. What should she say to Ruby? After Ruby had saved her? Zara couldn't read it because it was magic writing? Mmmm.

"Was it that magic ink?" Ruby asked curiously, and Lottie stared at her, her eyes wide with panic. Had she given herself away?

"I had some for Christmas last year – you know, where you get two pens and you can't see the writing until you colour on top of it." Ruby was giving her a bit of a funny look now, and Lottie nodded hurriedly.

"Yes, something like that," she agreed, and then changed the subject quickly. "I can't believe Zara always gets away with everything!"

Ruby shook her head disgustedly. "I know. It's so unfair. And somehow, all I have to do is say she's, I dunno, got the world's stinkiest feet, and half the staffroom's telling me that remarks like that can be very hurtful, and I need to channel my anger more constructively."

"They actually said that?" Lottie asked, grinning.

"Yup, Mrs Laurence, last term. She'd just been on a course, I think."

Lottie picked up a twig and poked it through the holes in the fire escape steps. "I don't suppose you'd like to come round after school tomorrow? I bet my uncle wouldn't mind. You don't have to if you're busy," she added quickly.

"That would be great." Ruby looked really pleased.

Lottie suddenly wondered if she'd been very lonely at Netherbridge Hill since Zara had got rid of her friend Lucy. "You know we live at the pet shop," she added, looking at the pattern of twigs again. She'd heard – she'd been meant to hear – quite a lot of nasty little comments from Zara's mates about smelly pet shops, and people who didn't have proper houses, and although she loved the shop, she suddenly wondered if perhaps Ruby would look down on it a bit.

But Ruby nodded excitedly. "I know, I've been there! I buy my lizards their crickets there, and these weird little things your uncle calls lizard treats. He told me once they were made out of mashed-up spiders, but I don't think that can be true. . ."

Lottie thought it probably was, and that Uncle Jack had just forgotten who he was talking to.

"Anyway, I love it there, and I've always been with Mum and she won't let me stay long enough to look at everything. Has he still got those gorgeous black kittens?"

Lottie smiled to herself. She knew exactly who Ruby meant, but she would have described them rather differently. The evil little fiends, probably. "He's sold two of them, but we've still got Selina and Sarafan, the girls." An elderly witch had bought Midnight and Jet, and promised Uncle Jack she would have their manners sorted out in no time, *she had her methods*. Lottie had never seen Midnight look quite so worried.

"You've got lizards?" she asked. Ruby seemed to be a very interesting person. Far too interesting just to have a hamster, she supposed.

"Two of them, they're brilliant," Ruby started to explain, just as the bell went.

They scrambled up and ducked out from under the fire escape. "Do you reckon Zara will do anything to us?" Lottie asked, trying not to sound nervous.

"Probably." Ruby looked mildly scared for a moment. "But then she would have done anyway, even if I hadn't pulled her hair, so I wouldn't be any more worried than normal."

Lottie nodded. That made a certain sort of sense.

Before she left for school the next morning, Lottie explained very carefully to the mice that she was bringing a friend home, and that they had to be discreet.

"We can be discreet!" squeaked the pink mice, who had now progressed to a six-mouse rodent pyramid on top of their cage. "We'll be as discreet as anything!" they added, dismounting and starting a conga line instead. "What does discreet mean?" one of them called back as the procession high-kicked its way down to the end of the shelf.

A disembodied voice sounded from Septimus the black rat's sleeping quarters. "They *really* don't know the meaning of the word," he called. "She means you have to be normal," he explained to the mice. "Which, considering you're pink, means you have to shut up and stay in your cage where no one can see you."

There was a meaningful silence as the mice digested this. Then the conga line broke up, and they trooped back up the shelf, looking woebegone.

Lottie felt terribly guilty. "It's not that I *want* you to," she tried to explain. "I love you just as you are, but it's like with the customers – Ruby doesn't understand what sort of shop this is. You have to be normal mice, the way you pretended to be before I knew what was going on."

The mice were pushing each other back into their cage, their tails and ears drooping. "That was torture," one of them muttered, then squawked, "Ow! Get your great big foot out of my ear, you elephant!"

"It won't be for very long," Lottie pleaded. "An hour or so. Ruby said how much she loves the shop, and she's so nice."

"They will be fine," Sofie said firmly. "And you will be late for school if you do not leave *now*, Lottie, go."

As Lottie grabbed her bag and her jacket, she could hear Sofie laying down the law to the mice. "You are *méchants*, all of you – oh, very well, you are *naughty*! Poor Lottie, you know how she hates that school; now she has found a friend and you cannot keep quiet to help her for a little while? After all those extra sunflower seeds she is giving you? Ah, yes, I have seen her! Ungrateful little beasts!"

Lottie wondered if Sofie had realized yet that *she* was going to have to keep quiet that afternoon as well. . .

But Lottie had misjudged Sofie. When she and Ruby pushed open the shop door later that day, they found a perfectly normal pet shop – although quite a few of the cages seemed to be empty, where the animals were too unusual to let themselves be seen. Lottie glanced quickly up at the pink mice's cage on the top shelf, and stifled a giggle. The cage was now apparently occupied by a pair of rather stupid-looking white mice, one of whom was wearing a sign round his neck that said "Really Normal". Lottie was pretty certain that the mice had cut the pictures out of one of the old pet magazines she had in her bedroom. She'd stopped buying them since she was surrounded by the real thing.

Sofie wasn't sitting up at the counter like she usually did. Instead she'd found a blue velvet cushion from somewhere, and was curled up on it daintily.

Lottie knelt down to stroke her, and said, "Sofie, this is Ruby." She really hoped Sofie liked her. She just hoped Sofie wasn't jealous. But Sofie thought-hissed, *Pick me up!* and scrambled into Lottie's arms to inspect Ruby properly. She perched her paws delicately on Lottie's shoulder, and gave Ruby her rather alarming smile. Then she said, "Woof."

Ruby gave her a slightly surprised look. Dogs did say woof, of course, but it didn't normally sound quite like that – as though someone who knew dogs said woof was trying to sound like a dog.

What is the matter? Sofie murmured in Lottie's thoughts. *Did I do it wrong? Did she not hear me? Shall I say it again?*

"She's beautiful," Ruby said admiringly. "Will she let me stroke her?"

Sofie inclined her head graciously just as Lottie said, "Probably. She's very friendly most of the time." She let Ruby scratch her ears and glared at Lottie.

Suddenly Ruby said in a horrified voice, "I've just thought, this isn't the dog who bit Zara and meant she had to have a rabies jab, is it?"

Sofie went rigid, and Lottie said, *"What?"*

Ruby grinned. "It's OK, I'm kidding. I mean, Zara is saying that, but I knew it couldn't be true." She held her hand out gently to Sofie again. "Sorry, little one, I didn't mean it. You knew I was being rude about you, didn't you? She looks ever so upset, Lottie, it's amazing. I suppose she's picking it up from you. You must be really close."

Lottie smiled, only half-listening. Ruby didn't know how right she was. "Zara's telling everyone Sofie gave her rabies?" she muttered.

Sofie snarled, very low, and Lottie automatically held her closer. "It's OK, Sofie, it's not true. It really isn't," she told Ruby. "Sofie tore Zara's skirt, that's all. She'd never really bite anyone."

Sofie huffed crossly. *Who says?* she muttered silently in Lottie's head.

"No one would believe Zara. Would they?" Lottie asked Ruby anxiously.

"We-eell. . . You know what school's like," Ruby admitted, giving Sofie a curious look. "Everyone just passes all the gossip on. And she did have a little scar that could have been a bite mark, but I bet she did it herself with lipgloss or something."

Lottie sighed. "Oh well. I guess everybody already hates me anyway. It's not going to make any difference. Do you want to come and get some biscuits?" She thought Sofie could probably do with one, after the rabies insult; she'd never seen her quite so shocked.

Sofie ate three chocolate biscuits, and glared at the kettle until Lottie made her coffee as well. She knew Ruby would probably think she was weird, but it didn't matter.

"She is such a cool dog," was all Ruby said, though, watching Sofie scrambling on to Lottie's knee, so she could lap her coffee too fast.

"You'll burn your tongue," Lottie muttered, but Sofie just gave her a dirty look. "She's, um, temperamental," she told Ruby, "but she is cool, definitely." She gave Sofie a little hug. "And not rabid. At all," she said firmly.

But Ruby wasn't listening. She was staring at the kitchen window sill, which was lined with pots of geraniums.

"Um, Lottie? There's a pink mouse in that flowerpot. . ."

7

The pink mice were in disgrace. Luckily Ariadne had popped in just as Lottie was trying to deny all knowledge of free-range mice in the shop, let alone pink ones. She felt incredibly guilty, because of course Ruby was right. The pink mice were just too nosy, and they'd wanted to get a good look at Lottie's friend.

Ariadne had smiled at Ruby, and stared at her very hard. The magic was so strong that Lottie could taste it in the air, a warm vanilla smell, like cupcakes. A gentle, warm sense of forgetfulness went with it, and Lottie had to work hard not to let her thoughts float away too. Ruby blinked at them both, and seemed to be thinking of food too. She just grabbed another biscuit without even asking, and sat munching it in a dazed sort of way.

Ariadne gave Lottie an amused look, and Lottie mouthed, "Thank you. . .!"

Ruby went home quite soon after that, but she did ask Lottie if she wanted to come to her house on

Thursday, the day after tomorrow, so the mice obviously hadn't ruined everything.

Lottie shut the door behind her, and leaned on it in a relieved sort of way. She could see why Danny had never wanted to invite friends back to the shop now. What would she have said if Ariadne hadn't turned up just in time?

Ariadne was talking to Uncle Jack by the counter. "You could have done that yourself, you know, Lottie," she commented.

Lottie shook her head. "That's too weird. . ." she murmured, giving herself a little shake. "I don't know what else I might have found."

"She seems very nice, though," Uncle Jack said hopefully. "Er, did you think so?" he asked Ariadne.

"Jack, are you really asking me if I happened to notice anything in Lottie's new friend's mind that we ought to know about?" Ariadne asked sweetly.

"No, no, of course not!" Uncle Jack looked embarrassed as Ariadne, Lottie and Sofie all stared determinedly at him. "Well, only a little bit. You know. Something might have just popped out at you. . . Sorry," he sighed. "I just want her to be . . . you know . . . nice. After those other girls were so awful, I just want Lottie to find a good friend."

"She has me!" Sofie snapped. Then she gently

nudged Lottie. "But Lottie, think. Ruby *saw* that stupid little mouse –" there was an indignant scuffling noise from the top shelf, followed by loud shushing as all the other mice sat on him" – which means that even if she does not have any magic herself, she is still sensitive."

Lottie frowned, looking at the others. "What does that mean?"

"Well, your mother wouldn't have seen that mouse, Lottie, would she?" Ariadne smiled at her.

"Or if she had, she'd have convinced herself she imagined it." Uncle Jack nodded. "No, that has to be a good sign for Ruby."

Lottie made a face. "I suppose so. I wanted to hide under the table when she said that, though. I just didn't know what to do!"

Ariadne looked serious. "I know you were caught by surprise, but you *will* have to use your power sometime, Lottie," she said gently. "Because if you don't want to, why am I teaching you?" She walked to the door, and Lottie was left staring after her, suddenly feeling as though it was hard to breathe.

Uncle Jack just sighed, and shut himself away in the little room off the kitchen where he made his special concoctions, like Ruby's lizard treats, and Lottie and Sofie were left looking at each other worriedly.

"What did she mean?" Lottie asked. "Sofie, do you think she's going to stop teaching me?"

"I do not know," Sofie murmured, looking out of the shop door, as though she could still see Ariadne. "I do not think she would do that. But maybe she feels she is wasting her time?"

"I didn't mean this to happen. . ." Lottie slumped on to one of the kitchen chairs. "When they said I'd inherited Dad's magic, I just thought it would be brilliant. You know. . ."

Sofie just looked at her with her head on one side, expectantly.

"Oh, I don't know what I thought. That things would be . . . easier, maybe. And they're not at all!"

"You wanted to just click your fingers and have everything perfect?" Sofie wrinkled her nose, as though she thought this was silly.

"There's no need to sound quite so sniffy about it," Lottie muttered. "I didn't even know magic existed until about two months ago."

"Ahem." A tiny cough interrupted them. All six of the pink mice had appeared in the kitchen, looking guilty. Most of the rest of the mice in the shop were gathered round the kitchen door, peering in.

"Sorry, Lottie," the pink mice chorused. And the one in front added, "We'll be discreet *next* time, honestly."

Sofie growled menacingly. "I could gobble you up,

you know. All of you would be just a delicious little snack." She licked her lips threateningly, and the mice took several steps backwards.

"She doesn't mean it," Lottie said wearily.

Sofie shot her a disappointed look. "Lottie! I could have got them to behave for weeks! What a waste."

Lottie smiled at the mice, who were still backing slowly out of the kitchen. "Don't worry," she sighed. "If Ruby remembers anything at all about this afternoon, I think it'll be a miracle. She looked really woozy." Then she straightened her shoulders, a determined look on her face. "Sofie, I've got an idea. Come on." She took the stairs at a gallop, and shut her bedroom door tightly after Sofie whisked in.

Sofie leaped on to the bed looking excited. "What is it?" she asked eagerly. "*Vite*, Lottie, quickly, I am all ears!" She flapped her rather large dachshund ears as she said this, and Lottie collapsed into giggles.

"What is it now?" Sofie asked snappishly. "Come on, Lottie!"

"Sorry," Lottie gasped. "I'm a bit stressed out, and it was so funny, your ears – oh, don't worry. Look, Ariadne wants us to start using our training, she made that clear enough. So why don't we? I'm not ready to do something off the top of my head, you know, in an emergency like this afternoon. But we could do a spell between us now, couldn't we? Just to try? Something more than just the silly stuff we've already tried. I mean, you can levitate chocolate into your mouth beautifully, but I'm talking about something a bit more complicated."

Sofie nodded enthusiastically. "Yes! Yes, Lottie! Let us do it now!" Then she wrinkled her nose, and shrugged expressively. "But *what* shall we do?"

Lottie looked at her seriously. "I want to try and do something about Zara. She is *so* mean, Sofie. You've met her, you know what she's like. Well, if anything, she's even worse at school. And no one does anything."

Sofie nodded seriously. "She is very mean, Lottie. I think we should teach her a lesson, most definitely. What shall we do?"

"I don't know, that's the problem. We don't know how to do it, either. Do we just think about it and it happens? That's how it's worked before."

Sofie frowned. "Let us try." She climbed into Lottie's lap, and Lottie wrapped her arms round the furry little body, feeling the magic bond between them leap into life at their touch.

It was still so exciting to feel the magic bubbling through them, dancing in her fingertips and Sofie's whisker-ends. It was still very new, but Lottie didn't think she would ever grow tired of it. She couldn't understand why Danny didn't bother to use his magic. How could he bear to leave it lying dead inside himself?

Sofie shook her ears impatiently, telling Lottie to get on with it. *I want to see what we can do!*

Eagerly, Lottie searched her mind for Zara. She knew from her lessons with Ariadne that she could use her powerful feelings to make things *happen*. And the stronger the feelings, the stronger the magic. She didn't have to look far. The memories were there, at the surface of her mind, painful and scary. Zara teasing her at school. Zara and her gang chasing her through the streets of Netherbridge. The joyful fizzing in her blood seeped away, and the magic seemed to fade again as the memories took over Lottie's mind, making her feel small and stupid.

Lottie, stop it! Sofie shouted silently in her head. *Don't let her do this to you. Be strong, she's only in your mind! She's not real. Listen. . .*

Lottie jerked slightly as she felt Sofie's thoughts about Zara flowing into her own. The little dog was far more bloodthirsty than she was. Her memories of Zara's attack on Tabitha were furious, and exciting, and all mixed up with *cats* too. Feeling strong and confident again, Lottie laughed aloud as she felt Sofie's satisfaction when Zara's skirt ripped and Zara shrieked with horror. Her own fear of Zara and her gang seemed to swirl into the dangerous, heady mixture. It had been so *exciting* to attack Zara. Perhaps they could do it again? Lottie and Sofie smiled together, showing their teeth, wanting to bite and make her squeal. . .

They reached out into the night, searching, picking up other thoughts along the way. People were angry, and sad, and hurt, and Lottie and Sofie grew stronger. *Now where was Zara?*

"Ow!" Lottie yelped, and looked down, the fever leaving her eyes.

"Ohhh, what is it, what has happened?" Sofie growled, shaking her head backwards and forwards as though she was trying to empty it out. "Oh! Lottie, what did we do?"

"Don't eat us! Lottie, don't let her eat us!" The two pink mice shot under Lottie's pillow, squeaking frantically.

"I won't, I won't. Did you just *bite* me?" Lottie stared at the tiny bead of scarlet blood on her thumb in disbelief.

The mice crept out. "Um. Yes. But we didn't know what else to do," one of them explained.

"You were scary!" The second mouse was clutching her tail for comfort, twisting it between her paws.

"Sorry, Lottie. Er. Again. We tried shouting, but you didn't hear."

"I don't think you were there," the second mouse said nervously.

"It smells bad in here," Sofie muttered. "I know that

smell. Where do I know that smell from?" She scrabbled angrily at the duvet with her claws. "Ah, what is it?" Then she stopped, and looked blankly at Lottie, her dark eyes wide.

Lottie nodded. "The enchantress."

"You smell it too?" Sofie asked in surprise.

"No, but I can feel it. I feel like I should wash, like I'm all sticky with something sweet and horrible." Lottie held out her hands, turning them over, checking that they really were clean. The taint of wrong magic was only in her head. She shuddered. "Sofie, that was *us*. We nearly did something awful."

Sofie scowled, her muzzle wrinkling up. "We were only trying to do something about Zara. She is awful too."

"I know. It doesn't seem very fair." Lottie sighed. "Ariadne did say that the line between good and bad was difficult to see sometimes. But I don't know how we're supposed to do *anything* if it's that hard. How are we going to know?"

"We could bite you again!" the pink mouse put in helpfully.

"Our pleasure!" the second mouse nodded.

Sofie gave them a dirty look, but Lottie scooped the mice up gently. "Wait a minute. How did you know to bite us that time? Could you smell it, like Sofie?"

The mice shook their heads. "It wasn't the smell. You looked funny."

"You didn't look like you. We were scared, and we wanted the real you back." They shivered. "Don't go away again, Lottie, please."

Lottie stroked the tops of their heads, very gently. "I'll try not to, I promise." She sighed. "Maybe we just did it the wrong way?"

Sofie looked uncomfortable. She pawed at the duvet again. "We do not like Zara. I know we said we were not just doing it for us, but. . . We *really* do not like her, Lottie. I think that is why."

They stared gloomily at each other.

The pink mice scurried down the bed, and disappeared through a crack in the skirting board. They came back a couple of minutes later, heaving a slightly battered-looking Mars bar. They dropped it in front of Lottie and Sofie, panting. "We borrowed this from Danny's bedroom, ages ago. We've been saving it for a special occasion, but we think you need it now."

Sofie stared at the mice. "You are forgiven," she said grandly. "Lottie, open it."

"So we have to be only thinking nice things about people whenever we want to do any magic," Lottie said a couple of minutes later, licking chocolate off her fingers. She wrinkled her nose disgustedly. "That means no spells at school ever, then. I know this makes me sound like a spoilt brat, but it's so unfair! All I wanted to do was. . ."

"What?" Sofie asked. "We did not decide."

Lottie looked a bit embarrassed. "I was kind of hoping she might turn into a frog. Not for ever. You know. Just long enough to make her sorry."

Sofie sniggered. "A frog!"

"It's what witches always do in books," Lottie protested. She smiled to herself. "I really like the idea of Zara as a little green, ugly frog. . ."

8

Sofie wanted to talk to Ariadne about their near-disaster, but Lottie was too embarrassed.

"Not after the way she reacted to that enchantress. She hated her so much. I couldn't bear it if she felt that way about me."

Sofie snorted. "Lottie, we made one leeetle mistake! We are not evil enchantresses." But she smiled wolfishly. "I think I might *like* to be an evil enchantress. I would have a diamond collar."

Lottie gave her a doubtful look, and Sofie sighed. "You are so serious sometimes. Did you not enjoy it a tiny bit, Lottie? That flying feeling?"

Lottie shut her eyes tightly. "Yes," she muttered. "That's what worries me. I loved it, and I really want to do it again, but we mustn't!"

"So we have to ask her what we did wrong!" Sofie pleaded. "I want to fly." Her eyes sparkled. "Lottie, do you think that one day, we might be powerful enough really to fly, like Ariadne does? If cats can do it, then I should be able to, easily." She gazed dreamily into the distance, then snapped back to her normal self. "And I think we could have something much better than that scruffy broom. Maybe an armchair?"

So Lottie agreed to go and visit Ariadne after school on Wednesday. It was the first time she'd felt really nervous visiting the flat. She had a horrible feeling that Ariadne would open the door and just tell them to go away and stop wasting her time.

Actually the door seemed to swing open on its own, which was a bit spooky, but then Tabitha's face appeared round the edge. She was purring deeply. "I opened the door!" she told Lottie proudly. "I thought about swinging on it with my paws, and it opened. Come in; we hoped you might come today."

Lottie and Sofie exchanged relieved glances as Tabitha led them in to the kitchen. It didn't sound as though Ariadne had given up on them.

"I'm sorry I didn't. . ."

"Lottie, I'm sorry. . ."

Ariadne and Lottie both stopped, and Lottie said shyly, "Go on, sorry."

"I shouldn't have pushed you," Ariadne said apologetically. "You'll use your power when you're ready. I should have been more patient. It's only that I'm so sure you can do it."

81

"We did do it," Sofie said smugly. "We were fabulous."

"Sofie!" Lottie protested.

"Perhaps we need a very small amount of help," Sofie conceded.

"We nearly did something awful," Lottie told Ariadne grimly.

Shadow gave a low, purring chuckle. "Ariadne set her eyebrows on fire once," he confided. "You both seem to be in one piece, at least."

"So what did you do?" Ariadne asked eagerly, passing Lottie a glass of juice.

Lottie sighed. "We tried to do something – we weren't even sure what – to Zara. But it went really wrong. Suddenly I wanted to bite her, and really hurt her. The mice had to stop us; we'd gone bad, Ariadne. It was scary," she admitted quietly.

"But you stopped," Ariadne pointed out.

"Only by luck. We didn't stop ourselves. We were enjoying it." Lottie gave Ariadne and the others a worried look.

Ariadne shrugged. "You can make your own luck, Lottie. Besides, you know why it went wrong, don't you? That's why you're so embarrassed."

"Are you reading my mind?" Lottie asked suspiciously.

Ariadne grinned at her. "No, Lottie. You've got

bright red cheeks and you won't look me in the eye. Why would I need to read your mind?"

"Oh." Lottie looked up at her at last. "Um, yes. I suppose we do know. We were – well, I guess it was because we wanted to hurt someone."

Ariadne shrugged. "There you are, then. Evil magic."

"It is that easy?" Sofie asked doubtfully.

"Oh, I'm not saying it makes you a bad witch straight away. But it'll be even easier to do it next time, and the next time, and the time after that you won't even stop to think." She smiled. "But it's good that you enjoyed feeling your power. That can be scary sometimes. You just need to find a better reason to use it next time, that's all."

Lottie frowned. "It's going to be difficult deciding whether I'm doing something for the right reasons if I have to do it in a hurry," she pointed out.

"It shouldn't be," Ariadne said quietly. "It's no harder than deciding anything else. Think of it like deciding whether to say something mean to someone – except you're not just going to end up with someone not talking to you if you do the wrong thing."

"Or perhaps you are, if you have turned them into a frog," Sofie said brightly. "Because then they could only croak, is that not so, Lottie?"

Shadow made a disgusted noise, which sounded as

though he had a hairball. "Oh, Lottie, please. Couldn't you use a *little* more imagination?!"

Ariadne chuckled. "It sounds to me as though it would do Zara a lot of good to be a frog." Then she put her chin in her hands and gazed thoughtfully at Lottie and Sofie. "But it's worth remembering that you don't always need to use magic. Sometimes you can be stronger without it."

Lottie stared back at her doubtfully. She didn't think so. She wasn't, anyway.

"You don't believe me, do you?" Ariadne smiled. "Maybe you will one day. You don't need to be able to turn someone into a frog to stop them bullying you, Lottie. You just need to believe in yourself."

"But we can turn her into a frog as well, yes?" Sofie asked hopefully.

Lottie had been really looking forward to seeing Ruby's house. She definitely thought you could learn a lot about people from their houses – like her mum's flat was very white, and clean, and tidy (apart from Lottie's room, anyway). But then the pet shop was untidy, with cages stacked up everywhere, and things hidden in all sorts of interesting corners.

The first thing that struck her was how quiet Ruby's house was. "Wow," she said, as Ruby shut the front door behind her. "I thought with your mum

being an artist that your house might be a b⌐
paint everywhere and things."

Ruby looked round. "Nope. That's all in Mum's studio. Only finished stuff comes into the house; otherwise she'd never stop. She used to work in the house, but then I did some creative additions to one of her pieces when I was about two. With pasta sauce. She was not happy. It was after that she got the studio."

Lottie looked round. It was a beautiful house, although it did make her feel as though she probably shouldn't put her school bag down in the wrong place. Everything seemed so perfectly arranged, it would be a pity to spoil it.

Ruby grinned at her. "Don't worry, my room's not like this. We'll grab a drink and some apples or something, and then I'll show you my lizards."

Ruby's lizards were a bit of a shock. Lottie had been expecting something small and greenish and not very impressive, probably hiding under a rock. Instead there was a massive tank taking up most of one wall of Ruby's purple, glittery bedroom. In the tank were two large pale-blue lizards, both sunbathing under a lamp. One of them was lying on his back, his front paws folded over a primrose-yellow tummy. Lottie couldn't help laughing. He really looked as though he should have a newspaper over his head, and a Do Not Disturb sign.

As soon as they heard her, the lizards twitched irritably. The one on his front, who had all four legs flopped out sideways, opened one eye, flapped a leg at Ruby, and appeared to go back to sleep.

Ruby tapped gently on the glass. "Hey, wake up, guys, you've got a visitor," she said lovingly. "And I bet she'd like to give you something to eat. . ."

The lizards' eyes snapped open at once, although they made a show of strolling carelessly over to the front of the cage. The right way up, they were even more impressive, with darker blue crests down their backs, and long, scaly tails.

"Wow, they're beautiful," Lottie said, admiring them as they stared back at her curiously.

"They are, aren't they?" Ruby agreed, fetching a little box from a shelf above the tank. "That's Joe and that's Sam; he's a bit bigger. He always sleeps on his back like that. Do you want to give them one of these?"

The lizards gave up pretending to be cool and flung themselves against the front of the tank. Lottie could practically hear them hissing, "Feed us, feed us, please, we're sooo hungry. . ." She gave them a sharp look as she handed over the treats. In fact, *could* she hear them?

The lizards stared back innocently, mouths bulging with gungy lizard treats. They looked very exotic, Lottie thought to herself. She'd never seen

86

anything like them in her pet magazines, but their zigzag crests reminded her of Uncle Jack's venomous green lizards back at the shop. She gave Ruby a quick, thoughtful glance, but her friend was happily cooing to the lizards. She didn't look like the owner of a pair of magical reptiles – but then, how would Lottie know?

"I've never seen anything like them," Lottie told Ruby. "Where did they come from?"

"Oh, a big pet shop miles away. Mum took me, and I just fell in love with them. Do you really like them? Because I can get them out, they like exploring, but I won't if you don't want me to. Most people think they're a bit scary." Ruby looked at her hopefully.

"I like lizards. Uncle Jack's got some a bit like this too. They were probably asleep behind their rock when you came to the shop; that's what they do most of the time. He'd like even bigger ones, really, but he can't face having to feed them on mice. Will Sam and Joe let me pick them up?"

Ruby chuckled. "You gave them food. I shouldn't think they'll let you put them *down*."

She was right. The lizards swarmed lovingly into Lottie's arms and draped themselves over her as if they'd known her for ever.

"Ruby! Ruby!"

Someone was calling from downstairs, and Ruby

jumped up. "That's Mum. Probably asking about tea or something. You'll be all right with Sam and Joe, won't you? I won't be a minute."

Lottie nodded eagerly. As Ruby shut the door, she looked thoughtfully down at the lizards. What should she say?

They were looking back up at her curiously. Their strangely wrinkled scaly faces looked ancient and wise, and Lottie felt suddenly shy.

Then the bigger lizard, Sam, who was stretched out on Lottie's arm, closed one eye in an unmistakable wink. It made him look a lot less ancient and wise – more like a drunken uncle. Lottie gazed back at him suspiciously.

"Hey!" Joe had climbed up her other arm and was hissing in her ear.

Lottie jumped, and both lizards dug their claws in and cackled with laughter.

"You *are* magical! I thought you were! Does that mean Ruby is a witch?"

The lizards shook their heads vigorously. "No, no, no. But you are, aren't you?" Sam's voice was whispery, and it rustled like the wind blowing through dead leaves.

"We've not spoken with anyone in a long while." Joe nodded. "I'd almost forgotten how."

Lottie had a horrible thought. "Ruby isn't – she isn't – *bad*, is she? She's not keeping you here when you don't want to be?" She looked at the lizards doubtfully. They looked pretty happy to her, and she hated to think anything like that of Ruby.

"Of course not!" Sam hissed disapprovingly. "Ruby saved us. She's our little pet."

Lottie blinked. She wasn't used to thinking of it that way round.

Joe chuckled. "Poor little thing. She only came into that shop looking for a hamster. We had to work pretty hard on her. And her mother – wheew."

Lottie frowned. "Was it a magical pet shop? I didn't think there were very many of those."

Sam shook his head slowly. "No. We got lost. A mix-up with shipments on a boat somewhere – who knows? We ended up in a storeroom at this massive great 'pet superstore' – ha! – with a gormless teenager looking us up in a catalogue and trying to work out if we were geckos or iguanas. Us!"

"In the end they just stuffed us in a cage and conveniently didn't put a label on. Weeks, we were there."

The lizards shuddered expressively, their scales wobbling. Sam laid his head on Lottie's shoulder and hissed, remembering. "It was full of horrible little boys yelling, 'Mum, Mum, look! I want that one!' We had to do a lot of forgetfulness spells."

"You can do them by yourselves?" Lottie asked in surprise. Very few of the animals in the shop could do magic that wasn't just about changing their own appearance.

"Of course we can!" Joe said irritably. "What do you think we are, newts?!"

"Um, no. I don't know what you are, to be honest. A very rare sort of chameleon?"

"Oh, for heaven's sake," Joe muttered. "A chameleon. Do you know *nothing*, girl?"

Lottie tried to look apologetic, but the lizards were so funny. They reminded her of the old ladies who lived in her mum's block of flats, and were always grumbling about the lifts not working. "Sorry, I don't know a lot about reptiles yet."

"Well, for your information, I am not a chameleon, nor do I look like one," said Joe in a sort of sniffy hiss. "I don't have goggle-eyes, do I?"

"Stop moaning, Joe, you sound hot-blooded," Sam said calmly. "How should she know what we are? We're very rare, dear," he told Lottie kindly. "We're dragons."

"Dragons!" Lottie yelped, and both lizards laughed.

"Only small ones," Joe hissed, his head on one side, watching her with his bright black eyes.

"*Fire*-breathing dragons?" asked Lottie, awestruck.

Sam and Joe glanced at each other sadly. "No. Not yet, anyway," Sam sighed.

"We might be!" Joe said bravely. "We're still growing."

"I feel as though I *should* be able to breathe fire; I just haven't worked out how. . ." Sam mused.

Lottie frowned. She didn't want to offend the dragons, but she had to ask. "How do you know you're dragons?" she enquired delicately. "I mean, if you don't breathe fire?"

The dragons gave her a shocked look. "We just do," Sam told her in a gentle voice, as though she was a little backward.

"It's ancestral memory," Joe said kindly. Lottie could almost hear him saying, *Don't you worry your pretty little head about it, dear. . .*

"And the ancestral memory doesn't tell you about the fire?" she asked.

"No," both dragons muttered irritably, staring at their claws.

"Sorry," Lottie murmured. "I wasn't trying to pry."

"Don't worry." Joe wriggled down her arm, his claws scratching her very lightly, and lay on his side on the floor, looking tragic. Lottie almost expected him to put one foreleg up against his head and moan. "You're probably right. We'll never be able to do it. . ."

"Oh, I'm sure you will!" Lottie assured him, feeling guilty. "I bet you're right and it's just an age thing."

At that moment the door opened and Ruby came back in. Joe scrambled up and whisked himself under Ruby's bed. Sam just froze on Lottie's arm.

"Who were you talking to?" Ruby asked curiously.

"Oh, no one!" Lottie said quickly. "I mean, I was just talking to the dragons – lizards! Not that they were talking back of course; they wouldn't, would they? Um." She stopped, aware that Sam was looking at her, rolling his eyes, and shaking his head slowly in disgust. Joe seemed to be chuckling to himself under the bed. Lottie felt her face flush pink.

Ruby eyed her, obviously not knowing quite what to say. Lottie thought she could probably tell that something was going on, but she had no idea what. "My mum wanted to know if you'd like to stay for tea," she said, rather awkwardly.

Lottie thought quickly. She wasn't sure she could manage to sit through tea feeling this confused and not say anything that was actually fatally stupid, instead of just weird. She stood up, carefully unhooking Sam. "I really would like to," she said truthfully. "But I didn't tell Uncle Jack I was coming for tea, just that I'd be a bit late." Which was also true, but she could perfectly easily have phoned him.

"Oh, OK." Ruby sounded hurt, and Lottie wished she could tell her what was going on. But after the effort Uncle Jack and Danny had gone to keeping the secrets behind the pet shop from Lottie, how could she go and blurt it all out to someone else? She really needed to talk to Uncle Jack. Now.

After an uncomfortable goodbye to Ruby, she

dashed home, almost colliding with Danny in the shop doorway.

"Look where you're going!" her cousin muttered, but Lottie got the feeling he wasn't paying proper attention to her. There was a strange look on his face: worried, excited, a little scared. His eyes flickered over her and then moved on, as though he couldn't concentrate.

"You've been doing magic, haven't you?" Lottie demanded accusingly.

"What if I have?" Danny answered, seeming to come out of his daze for a moment.

"You look weird," Lottie said, as she pushed open the door. "I just hope you haven't been doing anything stupid," she added severely.

Danny took enough notice of Lottie to make sure he looked normal while he was talking to his dad. Lottie almost wished she hadn't warned him. But at the moment she was too worried about her own problems to fuss about Danny for long. He was a year older than her, and much more experienced at living with magic. He would be able to look after himself. Besides, Sofie had been sure he was just messing around.

Sofie came trotting into the shop to see her as Danny vanished upstairs with Septimus, the black rat. "What was Ruby's house like?" she asked interestedly.

"Oh! Yes, did you have a good time, Lottie?" Uncle Jack looked at his watch. "I thought you might stay longer?" he asked doubtfully.

"I couldn't! Uncle Jack, Ruby's got dragons in her bedroom!"

9

Everyone blinked at her, and Lottie sighed. "Honestly. I'm not crazy. Well, they said they were dragons, and what do I know?"

"What did they look like?" her uncle asked eagerly.

Lottie described Sam and Joe as well as she could, but Uncle Jack insisted on dragging out an ancient-looking leather-bound book, which was full of hand-coloured drawings of different lizards.

"Just be gentle with it," he begged. "And you mice, just leave it alone; it's absolutely priceless, and I don't care if the colours do look delicious."

Several mice who had been happily sniffing the binding backed off in a huff.

"Ahem! Can we see?" called Uncle Jack's own lizards. Everyone looked at them in surprise, as they'd done very little but eat and sunbathe since they arrived at the shop. Pretty much all they'd said until now was "More" when they were being fed. Uncle Jack delightedly lifted them out, and they sat on the counter with Lottie, flickering their forked tongues at

Sofie and chuckling at her evident disgust. All the mice climbed back into their cages, and shut the doors behind them hurriedly.

"Sorry, Lottie," one of the pink mice muttered to her on his way past. "Those things just give me the creeps!"

The book was fascinating, but Lottie couldn't find Sam and Joe in it anywhere. Oddly enough, Uncle Jack wasn't at all disappointed.

"A new breed!" he kept muttering, watching the green lizards admiring their own picture and laboriously spelling out the description. "*Draco graci*! Or maybe *Draco netherbridgius*! I must see them, Lottie!"

"But that's the problem!" Lottie wailed. "What do I say to Ruby? She doesn't know what they are, and she heard me talking to them and now she thinks I'm mad!"

"Mmm. That is tricky." Uncle Jack sat down thoughtfully. "She saw the pink mice, didn't she. . .? So she's obviously got some spark, deep down. But is she ready to be told. . .?"

"She won't believe me," Lottie said sadly. "She'll think I'm stupid, or worse, she'll think I'm playing some kind of mean trick on her."

Sofie tapped her claws on the counter for attention. "Do not tell her, Lottie," she said firmly.

"But the lizards!" Uncle Jack protested, banging a hand on the counter. "I have to see them, Sofie!"

"Bring her here, Lottie. Do not tell her. *Show* her." Sofie put her head on one side, looking pleased with herself.

"Oh!" Lottie nodded. "But what if Ruby tells everyone?" She gazed round at the shop, at the towers of cages, all the animals watching and listening anxiously. "I mean, can you imagine what would happen?"

Uncle Jack looked at her seriously. "Of course I can, Lottie. Don't you think it's something we've lived with every day? Especially when we knew you were coming to stay here again."

"How can we risk it?" Lottie asked.

"You have to trust her, Lottie." Sofie nodded decisively. "Yes. If she is your friend, you must trust her. I know you do anyway."

Uncle Jack agreed, his voice serious. "She's right, Lottie. If Ruby isn't the kind of person we think she is, she just won't believe what she's seeing. But . . . it may make it hard for her to be friends with you afterwards. She knows something strange was going on, and you're right, she might think you're playing some sort of trick on her."

"She already thinks I talk to lizards," Lottie sighed. "When I said goodbye earlier she was really off with me. Let's go for it. I'll ask her tomorrow if she can come over – maybe on Saturday?"

*

Ruby seemed slightly doubtful when Lottie asked her, but luckily Zara gave one of Ruby's red curly ringlets a sharp tweak as she happened to be passing. It seemed to remind Ruby how much nicer Lottie really was.

"Um, thanks. OK. I don't think I'm supposed to be doing anything. I'll call you if my mum says no." It wasn't exactly the world's keenest acceptance, but it would have to do.

When Ariadne found out what they were planning, she said she'd come round too, just in case they needed to "help Ruby out" again. That was what she called it, anyway. Lottie was pretty sure that Shadow and Tabitha just wanted to see what was going to happen.

Ruby hadn't said exactly what time she would come on Saturday, so Lottie had to hang around the shop, trying to be busy – there was no point in doing her homework; she'd already tried to do her maths and then realized she'd spent twenty minutes doing the wrong page from the book. Uncle Jack had let Selina and Sarafan out for a walk round the shop – first making them promise not to even go near the mice. It had been Selina, sitting on top of Lottie's homework diary, who had gleefully pointed out that she wasn't doing the right problems. "*And* you've got them wrong," she added, in a smug little voice, reading Lottie's maths book upside down.

Lottie glared at her, and Sofie trotted back across the shop from where she'd been chatting with Septimus the rat. "Pick me up!" she yapped, scratching Lottie's leg. "She's right," she told Lottie crossly, looking at her messy page. She hated it when the cats were right. "How long have you been sitting there? Couldn't you have told her before?"

"She needed the practice anyway," Selina said, languidly licking a paw. "Her maths is *dreadful*. But then, what can you expect from someone who bonds herself with a dog? All dogs are illiterate. . ." Selina was still pretending to wash, but she was peering wickedly round her paw, waiting for Sofie to try and leap at her. She'd scratched Sofie's nose before, and she was clearly hoping for another chance.

Just then the door opened, and Ruby peered round it. Selina sighed dramatically, and did a graceful leap off the counter. It was clear that she wanted to show off. She was definitely concentrating on the delicate placement of her paws as she strolled towards the door.

Ruby looked less sure of herself than usual, as though she half-remembered the weird experiences she'd had here last time she came. Or maybe it was just that she'd come to visit her strange friend who talked to lizards. . .

Just as Lottie thought that, Ruby's bag wriggled, and a claw stuck itself out from under the flap and waved. Sam poked his head out and winked. Selina's pretty black face wrinkled in disgust, and she stalked haughtily into the far room where the cat pen was. Only Lottie heard her hiss, "Reptiles. . ." in disgust. Lottie wasn't sure if Sam and Joe had stowed away, or if Ruby had brought them for moral support. She didn't think Ruby would carry them in such a little bag, though. They had to be sitting on each other's tails.

Lottie nudged Uncle Jack, who hadn't noticed, and his eyes lit up.

"Hi Ruby! Do you want a drink? We could get some juice and I could show you all the animals. . ." Lottie suggested, trying to sound super-normal, and thinking, *Well, all the ones that aren't invisible at the moment. . .* It didn't help that while she and Ruby were getting drinks in the kitchen, Uncle Jack was tiptoeing round them, trying to get behind Ruby so he could peer into her bag and get a better look at Sam and Joe. He kept pretending to need to open cupboards, but he was a terrible actor. Eventually Sofie pulling discreetly on his trouser leg worked, and he backed reluctantly out of the room.

Lottie hadn't really decided how she was going to tell Ruby about the shop; she was planning just to see what happened, but the atmosphere felt so weird. She and Ruby were hardly talking, and Lottie felt like the secret was actually weighing down on her, squashing her so she couldn't talk properly. She couldn't bear it any longer. She handed Ruby a glass of orange juice. "It's OK, stay there, I've just got to get something," she muttered quickly, and she ran back into the shop, ignoring Uncle Jack's frantic signals for an update. She climbed up the stepladder to the pink mice's cage, where they were obediently hiding. "Hey, do you want to come and meet Ruby?" she asked quietly.

"Did you tell her already?" one of the mice, the one Lottie called Fred, squeaked. "We didn't hear! What did she say?"

"No, no, I haven't. I can't think how to tell her, so I just want her to meet you, is that OK?"

"Oooh, yes, please!" and he scrambled out of the cage and into her hand, leaving all the others grumbling about how it wasn't fair, especially as it had been Fred last time as well.

"Sssshh! Hopefully you can all talk to her in a minute, anyway. But I want to start with just one of you."

Lottie took a deep breath, and walked back into the kitchen, cupping Fred in her hands.

Ruby looked up at her awkwardly, and then she nearly choked on her juice. "He *is* pink!"

"You remember!" Lottie gasped.

Ruby was shaking her head and staring, her eyes huge. "Did you paint him that colour. . .?" she murmured dazedly.

"Do you remember seeing this mouse last time you came?" Lottie asked urgently, letting Fred jump on to the table and walk closer to Ruby. "I know I'm being really strange, but it's important! Please!"

Ruby shrugged, staring hard at Fred. "I think so. I do and I don't. I keep dreaming about him, and . . . and some flowers."

Lottie nodded. "The geraniums. Over there." She pointed to the window sill.

"They clash with my fur," Fred said kindly. "I expect that's why you keep dreaming about it; it's an *awful* colour combination, scarlet and pink. A nightmare, I'd say."

Unsurprisingly, Ruby didn't say anything. She just looked. Then she stood up, grabbed her bag, and made for the door.

But Lottie jumped in front of her. "Sorry!" she gasped. "Fred, you weren't supposed to talk! Not yet, anyway. Ruby, please sit down. I'm not playing a trick on you, he really *does* talk. That's why I asked you to come, because I wanted to show you what the shop's really like. I haven't told anybody before; it's a bit difficult to know what to say!"

Ruby turned round slowly and stared at her. "So what happened before?" she asked, sounding really hurt. "I did see him last time I was here, and you did something to me! You – you wiped my brain, or something!"

"No, that was me." Ariadne had suddenly appeared in the kitchen, so quickly that even Lottie blinked. Ruby was dumbstruck. Had she magicked herself into the kitchen somehow?

"You?" Ruby murmured. Ariadne was looking as witchy as she ever did, in a long black dress, her fabulous red hair trailing down her back. Apart from the lack of warts and dirty hooked fingernails, she was a typical witch. "Who *are* you?" Ruby stammered.

"Oh, I'm training Lottie," Ariadne explained casually. "She's my apprentice."

"You're an apprentice witch," Ruby said in a flat voice to Lottie.

Lottie could only manage, "Um" in a vaguely agreeing tone. She found it difficult to believe as well. Ariadne had never directly said it before.

"I had to do it, Ruby, I'm really sorry," Ariadne purred, moving closer to Ruby and laying a hand gently on her arm. Her eyes were suddenly such a bright green, it was impossible to look away. . .

"Don't!" Lottie flushed as Ariadne gave her a shocked look, breaking her hold on Ruby. "Sorry. But please don't force her mind again. I want to persuade her. Properly. She's my friend."

Ariadne shrugged. "If you must, Lottie. Come and see us tomorrow."

Shadow chuckled from the doorway as they

strolled out. "The young are so full of righteousness sometimes. Everything's so black and white for you, Lottie."

Ruby gaped at him – the old black cat, his muzzle grey with age, talking. Then she jumped as Fred scrambled on to her arm.

"Sorry," he muttered, as he scrabbled up her sleeve to her shoulder. "I don't like him. He was around when my cousin disappeared, and he always looks too hungry."

Ruby stroked him with the tip of one finger disbelievingly.

"Mmm, mmm, behind the ears, a leetle lower. . ." Fred wriggled delightedly. "Oooh, now you're tickling!"

"Oi! She's ours!"

Ruby was still wearing her bag – she hadn't relaxed enough to take it off – and Sam and Joe were now speedily climbing out of it.

"Aaaargh!" Fred gave a terrified shriek, and leaped from Ruby's shoulder to the table, then ran to hide shuddering inside Lottie's jumper.

Ruby was almost as surprised as he was. Her eyes were so wide that Lottie could see a ring of white all round, and she seemed to have stopped breathing.

Sam crawled on to her shoulder and peered up at her. "Breathe, dear," he said firmly.

Ruby gulped air.

"Hey Lottie!" Joe said, putting his forelegs on the table. "Got any lizard treats?"

"We fancied a trip, so we thought we'd come and see you too. No problem to climb into that bag," Sam explained airily. "Ruby, stop shuddering, I'm going to fall off. Calm down, my pet."

"But you talk!" Ruby moaned. "And you understand! I've probably told you things I didn't want *anybody* to know."

Sam closed one eye in a slow wink. "I'll take your secrets to the grave, Ruby. Just keep the lizard treats coming, though, eh?"

Ruby gave Lottie a panicked look. "Are all the animals in the shop like this?"

"Well, they can all talk," Lottie admitted. "But some of them don't say much. Sam and Joe are pretty special, though." She spotted Sam shaking his head, and realized he didn't want to hit Ruby with the dragon thing just yet. "Do you want to meet some of the others?" she asked quickly. Then she noticed that Uncle Jack was hovering hopefully by the door again. "And please could my uncle look at Sam and Joe? He really likes lizards."

"I've never encountered blue ones before," Uncle Jack said, gazing admiringly at them. "They're very rare, I'm sure."

Sam and Joe raised their crests proudly. "Oh, we are, most definitely," Joe nodded.

"Would you by any chance be a lizard *expert*?" Sam asked, trying to sound casual.

Lottie led Ruby into the shop as Uncle Jack and the lizards threw themselves eagerly into a technical discussion about flame production.

Now that Ruby knew the secret, all the cages were full again, as even the strangest animals could show themselves. The pink mice were sitting in a row on the shelf in front of their cage, dangling their tails and discussing Ruby's hair colour, and whether it was natural.

One of them leaned down and asked her curiously, "I've always wanted to know, what do you use to paint the freckles on with? Doesn't it run in the rain?"

"Um, no," Ruby murmured, almost apologetically. "I don't paint them on, I just have them."

"Oh, how disappointing! I was thinking you could do different patterns and everything, so exciting." He gave her a sympathetic look, and Lottie giggled.

"I do get more of them when it's sunny," Ruby volunteered.

"Oooh, like a sort of living weather forecast! How original!" another mouse said admiringly, and Ruby blushed.

"Look, now they've all gone!" Fred said, and the mice giggled hysterically, leaning on each other's shoulders.

Lottie giggled. "Come and see the kittens," she

suggested to Ruby, who was looking really embarrassed by all the staring mice. "You liked them before, didn't you?"

"Did she?" The mice looked really disappointed. "Thought she had more taste," one of them muttered.

"Ignore them," Lottie told her friend. Luckily Ruby seemed to be still so amazed by the mice talking that she wasn't really bothered by what they were actually saying.

Selina and Sarafan were lounging on top of their pen, now with Lottie's maths textbook open in front of them. "This is very easy, Lottie," Sarafan purred. "I don't know why you have such trouble with it. Hello, red-haired girl."

Ruby looked taken aback.

"Comparatively, she's the nice one," Lottie whispered in her ear. "I need that back, you know," she added to the kittens.

Selina gave a cat shrug, and her voice was extra purry as she replied. "You don't *really*, Lottie. You could just pick any numbers and write them down. Then just rub them out a few times for the look of it. You'd get more answers right that way. Anyway, where is your new magazine? I'm bored."

Ruby stared. "They're so mean," she murmured. "Are all cats like that?"

"Oh no, you saw Shadow and Tabitha, didn't you? They're lovely. Well, Shadow's a bit bossy. . ."

"You mean he's a rude old control freak," Sofie told her, smiling at Ruby and showing a lot of teeth. She made sure Selina and Sarafan got a look at the teeth too.

Ruby gave her a sharp look. She was starting to get over the initial shock of the shop. "*Did* you bite Zara?" she asked, almost hopefully. "Or was it lipgloss like I thought?"

"Lipgloss," Sofie nodded sadly. "Lottie's uncle does not allow me to bite. Except in Special Circumstances. I only bit her skirt." She made her mournful face, where her ears drooped and her eyes looked enormous, and Ruby crouched down to stroke her. "Well, I bet you could have done," she said comfortingly.

"Of course I could!" Sofie yapped. "You are a sensible girl; I told Lottie she was right to trust you." She closed her eyes blissfully as Ruby scratched behind her ears and gave Lottie a questioning look.

Lottie looked embarrassed. "She means telling you about the shop. And I know it sounds weird getting advice from a dog, but she's not a normal dog—"

"I am her familiar!" Sofie told Ruby smugly.

"What does that mean?" Ruby asked.

Lottie wasn't sure how to explain. "Umm. I suppose—"

"It means I tell her what to do," Sofie said matter-of-factly. "Lottie, do we have any more biscuits? I am hungry."

"Is it to do with – the *witch* thing?" Ruby asked rather nervously.

Lottie nodded. She was glad Ariadne had told Ruby that, because it wasn't the sort of thing it was easy to drop into conversation. "Sofie knows more about magic than me. I haven't been doing it very long. My mum doesn't believe in it, so I didn't know I could till I got here."

"Together, we are very powerful," Sofie gloated. "Lottie, biscuits!"

"A powerful force for biscuits. . ." a catty little voice sniggered, and Selina and Sarafan dived back into their pen, leaving Lottie's maths book with a suspicious claw-mark on the cover.

"I don't suppose you could show me some magic?" Ruby asked hopefully. "I mean, can you just do it whenever? Or does it have to be midnight, and in a chalk circle with a silver dagger, that sort of thing?"

"What have you been reading?" Sofie asked disgustedly. "Look."

Lottie hadn't really known what to say, but she felt Sofie pull power out of her suddenly. She gave a tiny gasp – it felt like being dizzy – and then Ruby gasped too, much louder.

Selina and Sarafan were yowling furiously as they floated above their pen in a whirling circle, nose to tail. "I have wanted to do this for so long. . ." Sofie said dreamily, her nose twitching as she swirled them around, faster and faster.

Giggling, Lottie pulled her power back, but gently, so that Selina and Sarafan landed softly back in their pen. Their black fur was bristling, their tails fluffed out to twice their size. They hissed and spat as they disappeared on wobbly legs into their sleeping box, threatening revenge.

"We should probably leave them to get over it," Lottie said. "You'd better watch your back, Sofie." She had to tow Ruby away; her friend was still staring mutely at the kitten pen, or rather the patch of space above it. It was sparkling slightly.

As they walked back into the main shop they found Septimus actually standing up for once, on top of his cage, trying to peer out of the shop window. "Lottie, do you know where Danny is?"

"No; didn't he say he was meeting some friends from school?" Lottie asked. "Why, are you worried about him?"

"No no," Septimus murmured. "I'd just like to know where he is, that's all." He was remarkably unconvincing, and Lottie looked anxiously out of the window too.

"Septimus. . ." Sofie's voice was a low growl. "What have you and Daniel been doing?"

"I did tell him to be careful." Septimus was

wringing his tail like the mice did sometimes. Lottie had never seen him look so worried. "Ah! Here he is!" he squeaked with relief, and scrambled down the shelves to run and meet Danny as he opened the door.

Danny looked a mess. His shoulders were drooping, and he had mud streaked all up his jeans and his best hooded top. He stroked Septimus, who had run up and perched on his shoulder, and was chittering lovingly and worriedly in his ear. "Hey, Lottie, hey, Ruby," he muttered. Which meant that something had gone very wrong; he was never usually so polite.

Lottie forgot about being cross with him, and went and grabbed three Cokes from the fridge. Uncle Jack was so busy measuring Sam and Joe's crests that he didn't even notice when she filched the biscuit tin. Then she and Ruby and Sofie and Septimus chivvied Danny up the stairs to her room. Ruby looked as though she thought she should stay behind at first, but Septimus muttered, "Bring her. She's sensible." Which was true, but Lottie did wonder if it meant he thought *she* wasn't.

"What did you do?" Sofie asked as soon as Danny was sitting on Lottie's bed, her whiskers quivering with nosiness.

Danny shrank. He'd obviously been working on twisting how people saw him, and he seemed to go further inside his clothes somehow, so that Lottie's eyes just slid over him, a pile of clothes on the bed. Then there was a sharp tug in Lottie's head as Sofie hooked her claws into the mist Danny had put in their minds, and jerked it away.

"Stop it," Sofie said sternly. "You cannot put us off with those silly tricks, even if they work on your friends."

Danny sighed, and wriggled, and was normal again. "They don't. That's the problem. Give us a biscuit, Lottie."

Ruby was watching with round eyes. "He can do it too?" she whispered to Lottie.

"He could if he tried," Sofie said. "But he is too lazy. And now he has got into trouble, mmm?"

"There's no need to sound quite so pleased about it," Danny said, but he sounded too tired to be cross.

"We aren't," Lottie assured him. "We were worrying about you, but I sort of thought you were bigger than me and you knew what you were doing—"

"Huh!" Danny's voice was bitter. "I wish."

Lottie had never heard him sound like this, almost as though he was going to cry, and she wished she could give him a hug. He wouldn't let her, though, especially not with Ruby there.

Sofie jumped on to the bed, her sharp black eyes softening, and laid her muzzle on his knee. "You are a very silly boy," she said affectionately.

Septimus eyed her suspiciously but didn't complain, and Danny put his hand on her back.

Lottie sent all her power to Sofie in a wave of reassurance, and Danny looked a bit less battered.

"Wow," he muttered. "I didn't know you could do that." He sounded impressed, and Lottie glowed inside. "It was those boys in my class," he suddenly burst out, and everyone tried not to look too obviously interested in case they put him off.

"Bunch of brain-dead morons," Septimus snarled. "They aren't worth it."

"Yeah, well, I should have listened to you, shouldn't I?" Danny sighed. He shot a shamefaced glance at Lottie and Ruby. "I was trying to make them like me. I worked a glamour, like I was asking Ariadne about, you know?"

Lottie nodded, but Ruby looked confused. "A what?" she asked, looking at Danny like she thought he was wonderful.

"It's like a costume," Lottie muttered. "Making people see things that aren't there. *Lying*, basically."

"Thanks," Danny growled. "Just because you can't do it. Anyway, it was working, I know it was. They were liking me, and they said did I want to come skateboarding with them, in the park, and I did. Only the glamour didn't work on skateboarding tricks. I was useless, and I fell off and it really hurt, and then the glamour stopped working at all and they all laughed at me," he finished in a rush. He sounded so unlike himself that Lottie almost wanted to cry too, she felt so sorry for him, even if he had been trying to deceive people.

Ruby got up and actually did go and give him a hug. Danny looked embarrassed, but a bit grateful, so Lottie hugged him too. Danny stood it for about ten seconds. "OK, you can all get off now," he muttered.

"Maybe you fell off because you were having to concentrate on the glamour?" Lottie asked, pretending the hug hadn't happened.

"Probably. It was really hard work keeping it up," Danny admitted.

"That is because you have no discipline, and you will not bother to practise," Sofie said in a very smug voice.

Danny shrugged one shoulder irritably but didn't say anything.

"You see, Lottie? All those boring exercises are worth it." Sofie tucked her tail round herself and sat up in triumph.

"He knows, you don't need to go on at him," Septimus hissed protectively.

"Huh." Sofie stared at the ceiling. "You should look after him better," she murmured sweetly.

Septimus nearly flew at her, but Danny grabbed him. "She's right, Sep, I should have listened to you. Come on, let's go down to the sweet shop and buy some peanut brittle." Peanut brittle was Septimus's favourite thing. "You'll have to go in my pocket, OK?"

Septimus nodded eagerly, and slid silkily in, tucking his tail away neatly. "I could do this in your blazer as well, you know," he said quietly. "I could come with you to school. You'd never have to be lonely."

Danny stared down at him. "'M not lonely," he muttered. "I just don't like being on my own all the time. It's different," he snapped at Lottie, who hadn't even said anything.

"But you shouldn't have to make yourself into a different person just so people like you," Ruby said unexpectedly, and Lottie felt suddenly proud of her friend. It was what Ruby had refused to do, all this time, to fit in with Zara and the other girls.

"Yeah, well, that's easy to *say*," Danny muttered, stroking Septimus's head, which was still sticking out of his pocket. "Sometimes it would be really great to live in a normal house, with a normal dad – and a mum – and do normal stuff!"

"But normal's boring," Ruby argued. "You and Lottie, it's amazing what you can do! How could you want to be boring like everybody else? Like me," she added, rather sadly.

"You're not boring!" Lottie protested. "And you stood up to Zara all this time, without even any magic to help. That's really impressive."

Danny snorted. "Yup. That's the one good thing about my new school. No Zara Martin."

"You wouldn't give it up, would you?" Ruby asked.

"He couldn't," Septimus whispered, but he was staring anxiously at Danny, his beady black eyes shining with hope.

"Could you really fit in my blazer pocket, Sep?" Danny asked quietly.

"If there was a piece of peanut brittle in there too, I could probably squeeze myself in." Septimus was trying to sound as though he didn't care, but Lottie could see his whiskers trembling with love. "And possibly the odd Polo too, for the good of my teeth," he was suggesting as he and Danny went down the stairs.

Lottie hung over the banister, peering after them anxiously. "Do you think he's all right?" she asked Sofie, frowning.

Sofie sighed. "Maybe. Maybe not. He has Septimus, and even though Septimus is only a rat, he is very sensible. Much more sensible than Danny. He will look after him. I like peanut brittle too, you know," she added mournfully, as though she hadn't finished the last box of French chocolates from Lottie's mother the day before.

"You don't think we should say something to Uncle Jack?" Lottie worried.

"Do you *want* Danny never to speak to you again?" Ruby giggled.

"Tempting. . . Yes, I suppose you're right. But I wish he was still at our school so we could keep an eye on him." Then Lottie started to laugh too. "I sound like his mum!" Then she stopped giggling, quite suddenly.

Sofie hunched her shoulders sadly. "Well, that is the problem, mmm? If she were here, perhaps he would not be like this. It is good he has us. Even if I do not think he will ever listen to what we say."

Lottie sank down on her bed next to Sofie and stroked her long ears. "I wish I could take you to school," she said enviously. "I wouldn't be scared of Zara at all if you were there too."

Sofie yawned, showing her beautiful white teeth, and the strange ridges inside her mouth. "I do not think I would like school," she murmured sleepily, curling herself into a ball. "It sounds boring. And smelly. But I will come if there is an emergency. I am going to sleep now. Wake me only if there is chocolate."

10

"Couldn't you use your magic to do something to Zara?" Ruby asked thoughtfully, as they walked to school on Monday. Lottie had stopped by to pick her up; Ruby's house wasn't far out of her way, and it was nice to walk into the playground with someone else.

Lottie shook her head. "We tried. It went a bit wrong. Me and Sofie got all mixed up together, and it was as if we were hunting her – not us exactly, but our magic. Fred had to bite me to make us stop. You're not supposed to use magic to do bad stuff to other people, or it twists everything you do, and I think you get twisted up too."

"Oh." Ruby kicked at a pile of leaves that had been gathering over the last few days – summer was definitely over. "I have to say, Lottie, that sounds totally unfair. What if Zara does something awful to you and you're trying to stop her? Isn't that allowed?"

Lottie kicked the leaves too, harder. "Who knows?" she said, a little crossly. It *was* unfair. "Ariadne said I ought to be able to tell what's right, but I think I might get it seriously wrong round Zara. I really enjoyed hunting her." She gave Ruby a quick, anxious, sideways glance to see if she was shocked. But she seemed sympathetic.

"I would too." She looked hopefully at Lottie. "You know, I wouldn't tell anyone, if you felt like going bad, just for a minute."

Lottie grinned. "You can distract everybody while I feed her the eye of newt then."

They'd reached the school gates now, and Lottie noticed how they both took a deep breath as they went in, psyching themselves up.

"Eye of newt seems a bit cruel," Ruby said thoughtfully. "I mean for the newt, not Zara. Is eye of newt really true?"

"I don't know," Lottie admitted. "I haven't got to that sort of spell yet. It's all just thinking magic at the moment; that and learning herbs. But you'd definitely have to catch your own newts, Uncle Jack wouldn't sell you animals for anything like that."

"Mouse-girl," Zara spat as she pushed past them, and Lottie flinched. Typical. In ten minutes' time she would have the perfect answer for Zara, but now she was tongue-tied, her heart thumping.

Zara looked back at her and grinned. "Watch out later, Lottie!" she said evilly.

"What's she talking about?" Ruby muttered.

"Probably nothing," Lottie said hopefully. "She's

just saying it so I worry all day. It's all a big trick." She nodded firmly.

Ruby looked unconvinced. "Maybe. . ."

If it was just a trick, Zara was a really good actor, Lottie thought nervously. Zara was worryingly happy about something, and she kept smirking and making little sniggering comments to her friends. Luckily, after Ruby had come back to school, Mrs Laurence had let Lottie move to sit with her, even though she'd seemed surprised that anyone would not want to sit with darling Zara. But they were still close enough to get the full benefit of Zara's meanness.

"At least she's stopping me worrying about that spelling test," Lottie whispered to Ruby at lunch time. Mrs Laurence had decided that after a couple of weeks back at school a giant test was in order, and she'd been making dire threats about people who didn't do well enough having to stay in at break learning words. Most of the class had spelling lists with them in the lunch room, and were testing each other.

Mrs Laurence was horribly cheerful when she came in after lunch. She beamed round at everyone. "Ready for our spelling test? Or shall we do some history first?"

The whole class howled, "Noooo!" and she laughed. "Sorry, I'll stop teasing you now. Get your pens ready. Zara, pass these sheets of paper round, please."

Everyone scrabbled for pens, and Zara came round with paper. She gave Lottie and Ruby a particularly nasty little smile as she gave out theirs, and Lottie wondered again if her threats had meant anything.

"Stop chattering, all of you, and stop making such a fuss, please, Aidan and James; you've had that spelling list for over a week, you've had plenty of time to learn it."

Lottie had been especially nervous because this was the first test she'd had at Netherbridge Hill – so far most of the work hadn't been much harder than last year at her old school, but she'd been worried that Mrs Laurence was going to give them a really difficult load of words. But actually, it wasn't too hard. She was very grateful to Horace, though. She'd been trying to learn the spellings in the shop yesterday afternoon, and she'd been muttering to herself, not realizing that he was looking down over her shoulder from his perch.

"You must know all of those by now," he'd snapped at her sharply.

Lottie looked up. "I think I do," she said worriedly. "But Uncle Jack's too busy to test me. He's got a new mouse delivery, and they're all travel-sick."

"Squeaky little fussers," Horace muttered irritably. "I'll test you. Give me the list. Hurry up, girl!"

Lottie did as he said. Horace was elderly, and grumpy, but he was very good at words – he always helped Uncle Jack with the crossword. She should have thought of asking him to help before. She passed the list over, and he straightened it out with one nobbly grey claw.

"Ridiculously easy. You should be on Latin verbs at your age. Pah! Right. Spell 'extremely'. . ."

Lottie smiled to herself as Mrs Laurence read out "extremely" as well. She didn't notice that Zara was smiling too, a nasty, sly, secretive little smile that didn't bode well for Lottie at all.

Lottie was just trying to remember whether she needed two e's or three when she noticed that Zara was flapping her arm in the air. What was she doing? Mrs Laurence wasn't going to be happy about her interrupting the test.

"What is it, Zara?" Mrs Laurence asked sharply.

Zara's face was angelically serious. "I'm sorry to interrupt, Mrs Laurence, but I think Lottie's cheating," she said, her blue eyes wide and worried.

Lottie gasped, and there was a low buzz of whispering all round the classroom.

Mrs Laurence looked at Zara, then at Lottie. "Nonsense, Zara," she said firmly, and the thudding in Lottie's chest subsided slightly. But not much. This was what Zara had been threatening earlier, which meant she had to have something better planned than just whining to Mrs Laurence. She exchanged a panicked look with Ruby.

"Quiet, everyone, let's get on," Mrs Laurence snapped, but Zara stood up.

"Please, Mrs Laurence, it's true! Lottie's got the word list taped underneath her and Ruby's table." Zara artistically allowed her eyes to fill with tears. "I saw her do it at lunch time and I told her not to, but she said she'd tear the covers off all my books if I said anything." And she cowered back into her seat, holding on to her friend Bethany's arm as though she was frightened. Bethany was trying to look serious, but she couldn't help smirking just a little at Lottie.

"I didn't. . ." Lottie said in a small voice, but she knew it was useless. Of *course* Zara would have taped a spelling list under her desk for Mrs Laurence to find.

Mrs Laurence sighed, and came over to check Lottie's table. She pulled out a taped-on list, and looked at Lottie sadly.

"I really didn't put it there," Lottie said miserably. She could feel the emotions in the room, so strong it was scary. Her own fear, Ruby's anger, Mrs Laurence's disappointment, and Zara's excitement. Suddenly she heard Ariadne's voice in her mind, clearly through the rushing swirl of feelings.

You will have to use your power sometime, Lottie. Or why am I teaching you?

And Ruby, only this morning: *What if Zara does something awful to you and you're trying to stop her? Isn't that allowed?*

It couldn't be wrong to stop Zara getting away with something like this, it just couldn't. But what was she going to do?

Suddenly Lottie remembered Tabitha's reaction when she'd told her and Shadow and Ariadne what Zara had done on the first day of school. Tabitha's memory of being tormented by Zara had been so strong that it had floated in the air like a picture. Lottie looked round the class. Everyone apart from Mrs Laurence knew what was happening, that this was all a great lie, and no one was doing anything about it. Except Ruby, Lottie realized, who was arguing with Mrs Laurence and being told to be quiet at once.

She smiled at Ruby. "It's OK," she said, ignoring her friend's glare and angry whisper, "I can't believe you're letting her get away with – oh!"

Almost before Lottie knew what she was doing, her anger and hurt had taken over. Magic was flowing out of her. She could feel Sofie, woken from a sleep back at the shop, standing up and barking her encouragement as Uncle Jack watched, amazed. Sofie was sending her power too, and her love, and her faith in Lottie.

A misty image grew in front of them, shimmering

in the air above the class. A picture of Zara, woven from the thoughts that Lottie hadn't even had to steal, because they were there for the taking on everyone's faces, in their clenched fists and frightened, angry eyes.

A true picture. Mean. Manipulative. A liar, a bully and a cheat. The image floating in front of Lottie seemed to grow almost solid as everyone in the class recognized it, and added to it. Even Zara, as she recognized the truth and hated herself. This time she was leaning against Bethany for real, her face white and sick – but Bethany was shrinking away, looking sick herself. The ghost-Zara looked so real, even Lottie was surprised. And now the image was changing, in a way she hadn't expected at all. It was moving. It had a piece of paper in its hands, and it was crouching down. Sticking the spelling list under Lottie's desk.

"I didn't do that. . ." Lottie muttered, half to herself, and half to Ruby. "I didn't know it would show us things. . ."

"Look at Zara," Ruby whispered back. "The real one, I mean."

Lottie glanced across, and gulped. She'd never seen Zara look less pretty. She seemed to have shrunk, and she had her hand across her mouth as though she was trying not to be sick. Suddenly, looking at her, Lottie realized what was happening to her spell. *Zara* was changing it, Zara and her friends. They were so scared that they couldn't help remembering the awful things they'd done. Their meanness was seeping back into the spell-image, making it show everyone the truth. And they couldn't stop it. "It's all coming to get them," Lottie murmured. "What goes around comes around. Just like the magic going wrong before. . ."

Lottie looked quickly round the class. "That's enough," she said quietly. Everyone knew now, and people were scared, and it wasn't as if she wanted to torture Zara . . . much.

Lottie reached out a hand, and snatched the spell-Zara out of the air, folding it down to nothing, like screwing up a piece of paper. It felt soft and light and hard to hold on to, like gossip. But Lottie held it tight, feeling it fall apart in her fingers. She blew the scraps out of her hands, back to the people who'd given her their thoughts.

Mrs Laurence gasped and then shook herself, as if she wasn't sure what she'd seen. "Zara!" she said in a horrified voice, and everyone seemed to wake up. They looked at each other, confused. What had been happening? Something weird. . . Zara had been mean to someone – that new girl, Lottie. But Lottie had fought back, hadn't she?

Lottie sagged back in her seat, exhausted. It had been a powerful spell, knitting together all those thoughts – and the pure nastiness of Zara had made her head ache. But she still smiled, feeling happier than she had since the first day she'd been at Netherbridge Hill. She noticed a few other shy smiles too, from girls who hadn't dared to speak to her before for fear of Zara.

Mrs Laurence put a hand on her desk, as if she needed to hold herself up, and murmured, "Zara. Yes." She looked at her favourite pupil, wondering quite what these strange memories that seemed to have arrived in her head were. "Zara, go to the office, please, and tell them to phone your mother. You need to go home. You look dreadful."

Everyone in the class stared as Zara crept out. No one was quite sure what had just happened. Zara was ill. Yes, that was it. She was going home. They were having a spelling test.

Mrs Laurence frowned down at the list she was holding in her hand – two copies, oddly. "Had we got to 'extremely'? Think carefully about how many e's, everyone."

Lottie finished writing it, her hand shaking. Then she smiled at Ruby. She had a feeling she would remember what had happened, even if the rest of the class had forgotten.

Ruby grinned at her. She'd gone so pale it made her freckles look darker. Then she whispered, very carefully, even though Mrs Laurence looked as though she wasn't noticing anything much, "But they've all forgotten! That's no use."

Lottie shook her head. "I think you remember what really happened because we know we can trust you. But Zara hasn't forgotten all of it. She knows something awful happened." She flicked a glance over her shoulder at Bethany, Ellie and the rest of Zara's little gang. "And they do too, look at them."

Ruby nodded. "I hope they're too scared to even go near you for a while," she hissed grimly.

Lottie gave a tiny shrug. "I wouldn't like to bet on how long it'll last. But even if they're mean again, I'll just be able to remember it. She's never going to scare me like she used to."

"You won, Lottie!" Ruby breathed, one eye carefully on Mrs Laurence, who seemed to be waking up slightly.

And Lottie nodded, grinning back at her. Yes. She'd won.

Sofie leaped at Lottie as she pushed open the shop door. "What happened? Tell me everything!" she barked, and there was a sudden clamour of squeaking and hissing and fluttering as everyone in the shop demanded to know more.

Lottie picked Sofie up and stroked her velvety ears. "Don't you know?" she asked, a little confused. "I thought you'd be able to see."

Sofie shook her head crossly. "No, not properly. You took all my power. I had to sleep all afternoon!"

"That's what you normally do," Uncle Jack pointed out.

Sofie looked at him as though he was an idiot. "Yes. But today it was not because I *wanted* to."

Lottie perched herself on the counter and described the Zara spell as well as she could. It took ages, because everyone kept interrupting, and then Danny came in halfway through and she had to start all over again.

"That sounds very powerful," Uncle Jack muttered worriedly when Lottie finished at last. "I'm not sure Ariadne should be teaching you that sort of thing yet."

"She did not teach us!" Sofie exclaimed. "We made it up ourselves. Lottie and me." Sofie was sitting very proudly on the counter. She almost looked bigger, she was so impressed with herself.

Lottie shrugged. "It was a one-off, anyway. Don't worry." She looked down at Danny, who was leaning on the counter, Septimus sitting on his shoulder. "How was school, Sep?"

Septimus's whiskers quivered in disgust. "How humans have the nerve to call rats dirty. . .!" He shuddered. "The toilets! And the history teacher was entirely wrong about the Black Death. Rats were not involved."

Danny grinned. "It was great. We've got this brilliant idea for science tomorrow. Sep's going to pretend to have escaped from the cage in Mr Jones's lab. The girls will go mental!" Then he looked down at the floor and muttered something, almost too quietly for Lottie to hear. "Thanks, Lottie. For yesterday. You're a much better mate than those prats at school. Or you would be if you weren't my little cousin, I mean."

Lottie sighed and Sofie rolled her eyes. For Danny, that was grovelling, but she hadn't expected him to admit even that much.

"And what happens if you get caught?" Sofie started to argue bossily. Lottie listened with half an ear as Sofie bickered with Sep, letting the warm buzz of noise from the shop drown them out. The pink mice were arguing about how to stow away in Lottie's PE kit so they could go to school too. Lottie made a mental note to shake out her trainers very carefully tomorrow.

"Are you OK, Lottie?" Uncle Jack asked. "You looked miles away."

Lottie smiled at him. "I'm fine. Uncle Jack. . . "

"Mmm?"

"Can I stay?"

Uncle Jack blinked, and Lottie felt the noise from the animals die away, leaving a hopeful silence.

"For ever, you mean?" Uncle Jack looked at her thoughtfully. He glanced at Danny, who nodded, and made himself very busy unwrapping a piece of peanut brittle for Septimus. Uncle Jack put an arm round Lottie, hugging her against his grubby old sweater. Lottie wondered if her dad had smelled like this, like hay and seeds and a faint pleasant whiff of dog.

"Lottie, love, I can't imagine it without you now. You know you belong here."

Lottie nodded. She could feel Sofie pressed close against her side, and Sofie's happiness doubled her own, over and over.

HOLLY WEBB is the author of the bestselling
Lost in the Snow and its sequel, *Lost in the
Storm*, as well as the popular Triplets series.
She has always loved cats and now
owns two very spoilt ones.

Don't miss Lottie's other adventure!

If you have enjoyed this book,
look out for these too!

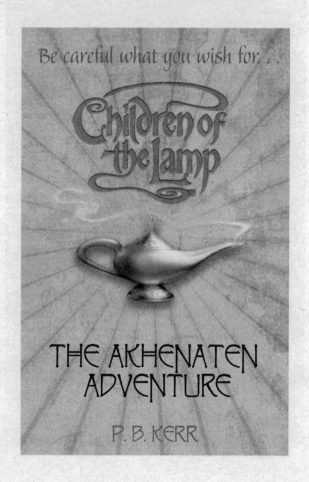

In the grip of magic!

Children of
the Lamp

THE BLUE DJINN
OF BABYLON

P. B. KERR

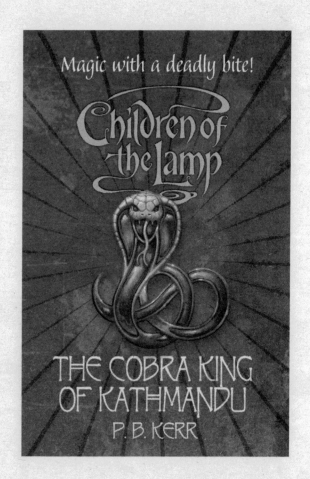

Magic with a deadly bite!

Children of the Lamp

THE COBRA KING OF KATHMANDU

P. B. KERR